Miss Ridley and the Duke
Copyright © 2024 by C. N. Jarrett. All rights reserved.
Published by Rogue Press
Editing by Katie Jackson

All rights reserved. No part of this book may be used or reproduced in any form by any means—except in the case of brief quotations embodied in critical articles or reviews—without written permission.

This is a work of fiction. Names, characters, places, and incidents are products of the author's imagination or are used fictitiously and are not to be construed as real. Any resemblance to actual events, locales, organizations, or persons, living or dead, is entirely coincidental.

This e-book is licensed for your personal enjoyment only. This e-book may not be re-sold or given away to other people. If you would like to share this book with another person, please purchase an additional copy for each reader. If you are reading this book and did not purchase it, or it was not purchased for your use only, please return to your favorite retailer and purchase your own copy. Thank you for respecting the hard work of the author.

Stay in touch through the C. N. Jarrett newsletter!

MISS RIDLEY AND THE DUKE

DAZZLING DEBUTANTES
BOOK ONE

C. N. JARRETT

To the amazing Mr. Jarrett:
Sixteen years ago we met and fifteen days later we married on a train platform with a license obtained the day before.

Taking a leap of faith with you was the most important decision I ever made. You have taught me kindness, supported my dreams, and caused me endless embarrassment by crowing my achievements to every pair of ears you encounter. You inspired the confidence I needed to write, so this book, in its entirety, is dedicated to you.

PROLOGUE

"When falsehood can look so like the truth, who can assure themselves of certain happiness?"

Mary Shelley's Frankenstein

∾

Annabel pressed her face against the mullioned windows facing the stable yard. She squinted to make out the figure riding up from the woods, frowning in confusion as she confirmed it was her betrothed, Richard Balfour. The Earl of Saunton had arrived early by at least an hour.

It was her rare use of this south-facing bedchamber that had allowed her to witness his early arrival. She had been exhibiting an uncharacteristic flash of vanity, twirling her new muslin day dress as she admired her reflection in the mirror. The embroidered gold flowers on the delicate ivory fabric suited her coloring and made her look softer … perhaps even pretty.

"You are no English rose, girl. I wonder if I will ever be able to marry you off."

Annabel shook her head to clear her father's vitriol from her thoughts. He was wrong. An actual earl wanted to marry her. Richard was her true love, and he saw her as pretty and captivating. He had stated as much when he had courted her before asking for her hand in marriage.

Chewing her lip, she tried to figure out what to do about her betrothed's early arrival.

"You are a hoyden, girl. No gentleman wants to marry a girl who rides in breeches."

Annabel again pushed back her father's caustic remarks. Richard liked to race her, and he had asked her to marry him while they had been out riding on the estate in those buckskin breeches. When he had inherited his earldom a handful of years ago, he had met plenty of debutantes in London. As a handsome and wealthy member of the peerage, he could have any young lady he desired—and he wanted her. To be chosen by him was the fulfillment of her dreams from the best part of the past decade. She was just nineteen and had never even had a Season, but she was preparing to marry the man she loved in just two more months. She was a success despite the baron's dire predictions.

Annabel glanced around the guest chamber at all the beautiful dresses of her trousseau. She would embark on her new life soon, managing the earl's household the way she desired and working with Richard to provide a school to his tenants' children. They would start a family. Her father, the baron, would be tolerated, but an insignificant part of her new life. Perhaps her brother might even visit and pay her mind as a married noblewoman. The future was so bright. Not every daughter of the aristocracy got to marry her one true love.

Annabel caught herself dallying and hurried downstairs to meet him.

∼

Thirty minutes had passed and still Richard had not called at the front door. Perhaps he was conversing with the stable master. However, it was Gibbons' afternoon off, so it was unlikely he would be in the stables when he could take advantage of such a fine day.

Annabel considered visiting the kitchens to forewarn the housekeeper that someone should bring tea as soon as Richard appeared. Then she would cut through the kitchen gardens and head to the stables to meet him. Her mind made up, Annabel set off to the servants' staircase.

It was about fifteen minutes later when Annabel entered the dim interior of the stables, her nose tickled by the fresh scent of hay as she made her way down the stalls looking for Richard. She started when she heard a strange moaning, like a cat keening in pain.

Horses nickered in protest as she hurried forward to the end stall to see what was making the strange sound, her slippers soundless on the hard-packed ground. She peered into the stall and then ... then her heart stopped in a painful spasm. Strange, the blood was rushing and pounding in her ears so loudly she was sure she would go deaf. How could one's heart stop and blood pound at the same time, she wondered to herself in a daze. As if from a great distance, Annabel observed she had entered a state of mild shock and took a deep breath to compose herself.

Caroline from the kitchens and Richard were engaged in

a passionate embrace, their mouths fused together as if they were one. It was highly inappropriate. Annabel did not believe it was suitable behavior for a man whose wedding was only weeks away.

Not suitable at all!

Something tore within Annabel's chest. She suspected it was her innocence shattering as her heart broke into pieces and her very life shifted into a new course.

Caroline moaned in the back of her throat, and Annabel startled back into the moment. An eerie calm descended on her as a bitter numbness spread through her limbs, accompanied by a strange, frantic energy that made her breathing quick and shallow.

"I apologize for my interruption, but I have a couple of things to say."

Everyone flinched in surprise, including Annabel herself. Richard and Caroline fumbled to right their crumpled clothing before turning to stare at her. Annabel realized she was the one who had spoken out loud. It would appear she was taking charge of the situation.

She looked to Caroline, who stared at her before bursting into loud sobs. Regretful tears streamed down her face. Annabel noted, with an odd sense of detachment, that it was not an attractive look as she continued to search for her own wits.

"I am so sorry, miss!" wailed the distraught maid.

Annabel drew a deep breath. "Caroline, I have known you since we were both young girls. You have been a member of our household for many years now. It is with great regret I must inform you that your services are no longer required." The girl's sobbing grew louder, a great noisy caterwauling that was rather unappealing.

You are in shock, Annabel. Your behavior is odd. Get this over with.

"Because of our long acquaintance, I would bid you to go see Mrs. Harris to request a character reference based on how you have executed your duties, the current circumstances notwithstanding. Inform her I would like her to assist you in finding a place in a new household as soon as possible. I will be along shortly to sign the reference. You are to depart Baydon Hall by the end of the week."

Caroline stopped sobbing, her blonde curls hanging limp after the storm of tears. She looked at Annabel with astonishment. "You would give me a reference?"

"Consider it an act of kindness. I detest the necessity of this conversation, but neither will I see you destitute, despite your disloyalty and lack of moral compass. I suggest you act quickly before I change my mind."

The maid made to leave, when Annabel realized she had a question.

"However, I do require something from you, Caroline."

"Yes, miss?"

"How long have you and Lord Saunton been … meeting in the stables?" Richard made a choking sound as Caroline's face reddened in shame.

"You mean *meeting* in the stables?" the maid clarified.

"Indeed. The emphasis is on meeting, not stables."

The maid looked down, shamefaced, to stare at the toes of her shoes. "About *mumble mumble*."

"What's that?"

Caroline squirmed. "About two months."

"Here in the stables?"

"See here? Is this really necessary?" interjected Richard.

Annabel turned to glare at him. He immediately

relented, staring in abashed fascination at the hay scattered on the ground beneath his boots.

"Caroline, here in the stables?" she repeated.

The maid nodded, keeping her face averted to the floor. "Usually. I would come wait here for him on days he was to visit, and he would arrive early, with the woods at the back to cover his approach, so no one would know what time he arrived."

Annabel's fingers and toes felt icy with shock as she digested this information. "Hurry along. Lord Saunton and I have private matters to discuss." She shooed the girl out, gesturing toward the stall door as she stepped aside.

The maid rushed out in apparent relief. Annabel did not blame her. She wished she could rush out and pretend she had not witnessed—nor heard—the past few minutes. Return in time and be back in the guest chamber trying on her trousseau—and this time fail to glance out the window. If she attempted to comprehend all the consequences of this moment, she felt it would tear her physically limb from limb. Her dreams for the future were lost. Her entire life changed in a matter of minutes.

Drawing a fortifying breath, Annabel turned to look at Richard. She was unsure what emotion she had expected to find on his face. Shame? Sheepishness? Tears would be nice. A fitting response to celebrate her loss of naïveté and the rending of their love. It was unexpected to find him scowling in defiance. He appeared to be blushing, at least.

"I believed a contemptuous father and an indifferent brother were the worst influences I had to contend with. Yet I discover a beloved's face can disguise a more awful character than anything I could have conceived of before this day."

"I never promised you love."

Annabel considered for a moment and knew she could not deny it. "You are right. You said I was pretty—captivating, even. You said I was one of the most interesting people you had met. Our long acquaintance, coupled with the marriage proposal and sentiments you voiced, all misled me into believing you loved me."

"I do love you, in a way. Just not the way you mean."

"But it is the way that matters! To me!" With that, her calm shattered, and tears rolled unchecked down her cheeks.

"Annabel, this changes nothing. I care for you very much. I want to make you my wife, any way you see fit. As my countess, you will have more freedom than this tiny world your father forces you to live in. It will be good for you."

"This changes everything! Our love? That was the most important part to me! I thought we would be partners, taking on life's challenges together. That we would make each other strong. That *you* were strong. But you are a weak man driven by base desires. If I do not help that stupid, naïve girl find a new place, what will happen to her?"

"She is a grown woman who made her own decisions." Richard's defiance had returned.

Annabel shook her head in disbelief. Just how many women had Richard been meeting since their betrothal had begun?

"I shall let the baron know to cancel our wedding. I could rail or scream, but I am not even sure where to begin. Good day, my lord." She turned to leave.

"Annabel." Richard grasped her arm. She looked back and found his expression belligerent, his stance stubborn. "I have no intention of allowing you to break the betrothal."

"What!" Her composure was forgotten as her jaw dropped.

"I want to marry you. Your father will agree with me. The baron will not pass up the opportunity to be closely connected to an earl. It saddens me you saw what you did today, but the wedding will proceed. The matter is out of your hands."

Annabel stared at him in wordless dismay. Tearing her arm out of his hand, she lifted her skirts and set off at a run to find her father.

CHAPTER ONE

"I am malicious because I am miserable. Am I not shunned and hated by all mankind?"

Mary Shelley's Frankenstein

∞

Josiah Ridley scowled at his daughter. "He is an earl, you ungrateful girl!" he bellowed. Catching himself, Lord Filminster lowered his voice. "My heartfelt regrets on finding your betrothed in a compromising situation, but this marriage will elevate our entire family within society. It will improve the chances of your brother making a better match. The wedding will proceed, Annabel. I will not discuss it yet again. It is time for you to accept it!"

Annabel, much to her shame, stamped her foot in frustration. It was pointless, as she was wearing slippers and standing on a thick, blue and yellow Aubusson rug that absorbed any sound her futile gesture might have made. "This is important! I cannot marry a man who engages in—

well, improper behavior—with our kitchen maid, no less, only weeks before our wedding!"

The baron bent his balding pate as he returned to his ledgers. "You chose him to be your husband, and I signed the contracts. I will not allow you to cancel the wedding with the earl. It has been set in place for months. He will advance our family's social status, and I will not alter this course over a minor indiscretion. It is unfortunate that you had to witness his lack of judgment, and Lord Saunton should indeed learn better discretion. But that is no reason for this level of upheaval. Good day, Annabel."

Annabel's mouth fell open at her abrupt dismissal. Her father scribbled in one of his ledgers, clearly indicating the discussion was over and her presence was no longer of note. Was she wrong to think Richard's behavior was unacceptable, or was her father so blinded by ambition that he felt no remorse about committing her to a miserable lifetime with a man of such low integrity?

She stormed out, slamming the door behind her.

Her father's muffled shout reached her as she fumed in the timbered corridor. "And change into proper attire, young lady! Breeches are for menfolk!"

Annabel swallowed a scream of frustration, her heart pounding so hard it felt as though it might burst right out of her ribs as she leaned back against the ancient marquetry to compose herself. After yet another argument with her father, she had to reconsider her options. Could she appeal to her brother? Brendan might have helped her out of this predicament, but he was off gallivanting in London with no expectations of his return. Even if she tracked him down, there was no guarantee he would take her side. Dearest brother Brendan had not visited her in four years, and because Richard was one of his closest friends, even he might refuse to intervene. Writing to him seemed utterly pointless.

Her aunt had been of no use either. Annabel had attempted a private discussion during her recent visit, but her aunt had scolded her for even broaching the topic and swiftly changed the subject to the trousseau. Clearly, the baron's sister would not be a source of aid.

With every passing day, the wedding loomed closer, like a spectral figure waiting in the shadows to harvest her very soul. Annabel stared sightlessly at the colorful medieval tapestries hanging on the opposite wall, chewing on her bottom lip as anxiety swirled through her thoughts.

The past month had been a parade of emotional highs and lows since what she now called *The Stable Incident*. She grimaced at the memory. After her father had confirmed Richard's prediction that the marriage would proceed, she had spent two days cloistered in her room, nursing her heartbreak. When her tears finally ran dry, an epiphany struck. Her heart could not truly be broken, for she had never known the real Richard—just the masquerade of a charming gentleman who had smiled and paid her attentions. Could she have truly loved someone she had never really known? Common sense told her no.

That realization became her impetus to rise from bed and plot to prevent the wedding.

She had started a campaign to wear down her father, pleading and debating, raging and reasoning with him week after week. Yet the baron, usually quick to yield when confronted with Annabel's emotions, remained resolute. His ambitions for the family's social standing had rooted him firmly in place, and he refused to be moved by the arguments she presented.

Her future hung in the balance. Marriage to Richard

would condemn her to a lifetime of the same loneliness and neglect she had endured since her mother's passing. How could she escape one cold, empty household, only to resign herself to another?

Oh Mama, if only you were still here!

The ache of loss struck Annabel afresh. Her mother's wisdom and strength had always been her solace, but now there was no one to offer her guidance. Within months of her mother's death, Richard had entered her life, and she had believed him to be her salvation. Now, that illusion was shattered, and she was left as alone as ever.

The irony was almost unbearable—once upon a time, Richard would have been the one helping her plot an escape. Now she stood, desperate to escape him.

Tears pricked at her eyes, but she squared her shoulders and blinked them back. There was no time to mourn her lost love with Richard. If she did not act soon, she would lose her entire future, and that would be far more devastating. What was a broken heart compared to a broken future? The first could heal, but the second would leave lasting scars.

Nay, she would find her path back to happiness—even if it killed her.

∼

"Mrs. Harris, what can I do? There must be a way to stop this wedding!" Annabel pleaded.

Mrs. Harris's expression was pensive, her brow furrowed, and her rosy cheeks had paled as she sat next to Annabel. It was against all propriety for a servant to be seated at the breakfast table, but Annabel had dismissed the footmen to speak privately with the only ally she had—

her widowed housekeeper. Mrs. Harris agreed the wedding could not proceed, and she had been like a mother to Annabel since her own had passed eleven years prior. Annabel did not care to let societal expectations interfere with their close relationship while her entire future was unraveling.

"Child, I am not sure. You say Lord Filminster simply will not reconsider ... perhaps you could convince Lord Saunton to call it off?" Mrs. Harris suggested.

"I tried. I begged and pleaded. I pointed out he could find someone more willing to abide by the sort of marriage he wishes to have. But he is so stubborn! He said it must be me. He complains he met dozens of debutantes over the past two Seasons, but not one whom he could mildly tolerate. He refuses to go searching for a new wife when he has already made his choice."

The older woman appeared to muse on this absent-mindedly as she picked up a flaky bun from Annabel's plate and nibbled on it. "Is there someone that his lordship—Lord Saunton, that is—might listen to? Someone who could convince him to change his mind?"

"Hmm ... that is a fresh idea to consider, but who?" Annabel tapped her teeth with her fingernail in agitation, thinking back on conversations with Richard over the years. After a few moments, she answered, "His cousin, the Duke of Halmesbury. Richard used to mention the duke all the time, although he has not in quite a while—"

"The Duke of Halmesbury, you say? Where have I heard that name just recently?" the housekeeper interrupted, a frown on her face as she searched her memory. "I know!" she exclaimed, startling Annabel as she leapt from her seat and left the breakfast room.

Annabel stared after her retreating form through the

open door as the matronly woman trotted down the hall. Glum, Annabel turned back to her plate of eggs, ham, and fruit. She forked up some baked eggs and brooded while she chewed, staring in bemusement at her china teacup.

She looked back to the door at the sound of Mrs. Harris's huffing return. The housekeeper was clutching a copy of *The Gentleman's Magazine* under one arm, her other hand pressed to her heaving bosom. Stepping back into the breakfast room, she turned and shut the door with a swipe at her perspiring brow.

"I found it!" the housekeeper trilled, resuming the seat next to Annabel.

"Found what?"

"The most recent copy of *The Gentleman's Magazine* has an article on the Duke of Halmesbury." Annabel arched an eyebrow. "Don't look at me like that, child! Lord Filminster discarded it, and Stedman reads it to us belowstairs, so we know what is happening."

"Well, show it to me, then."

"I don't know which page it is on. You will have to find it. These eyes are not what they used to be, and the letters are too small."

Annabel concealed a smile as she took the magazine and flipped through its pages. "Here it is! 'His Grace, the Duke of Halmesbury, renowned for his estimable charitable work, recently oversaw the renovations and restaffing of The Halmesbury Home for Children.' I wouldn't have thought *The Gentleman's Magazine* would print articles about foundling homes?"

"They usually do not, but His Grace is the most marriageable noble in the kingdom. The article is about him, not his works. Fathers such as Lord Filminster read it."

"Ah, fathers who need to marry off their daughters to

make important connections. I see your point." Annabel quickly scanned the article and looked up in excitement. "He is in residence at his country seat, Avonmead, in Wiltshire, to oversee the reopening of the children's home. That is just a day's ride from here, Mrs. Harris!"

"Aye, but a day's ride might as well be all the way to London, child. How will you get there to speak with him?"

Annabel chewed on a fingernail as she thought. "I could feign illness and take to my chambers. You could insist on bringing my meals to me, so we could pretend I am here while I ride to visit the duke. It will be a secret between you, me, and Gibbons. As stable master, he will have to hide the fact that I have taken a mount."

Mrs. Harris's broad face looked appalled, her horrified hazel eyes searching Annabel's face. "Have you gone mad?"

"Mrs. Harris, I can do this. I will dress in my riding garb with an overcoat and hat to ensure I appear to be a man. I will avoid other travelers and ride straight through to Avonmead. Then the kindly duke with the excellent reputation will send me back in a carriage. It is a minor risk to save my future."

Mrs. Harris looked uncertain.

"Mrs. Harris, if I do not find a way to evade this marriage, I will have no choice but to sell my jewels and run off to the Continent. Or travel north to Scotland to find an occupation."

The older woman hissed in horror, her face crumpling as she considered Annabel's words.

"And Mama would want me to be bold to save myself," Annabel added gently.

Mrs. Harris sighed, worry lines wreathing her face. "Aye, but she will return from the grave to murder me if anything happens to you." At those words, Annabel knew the housekeeper was almost decided in her favor. She waited in silence as Mrs. Harris continued. "We will have to imply it is your monthly illness, or his lordship will call for a doctor. If he thinks it is your courses, he will stay far away to avoid your feminine vapors, as he likes to call them. I could buy a couple of days if I shoo the maids away from your rooms and take your meals upstairs myself."

Annabel clapped her hands in delight and kissed the worried housekeeper on her plump cheek. "You are a treasure, Mrs. Harris."

"Aye, a treasure of a fool to even think about this. And I will be a fat fool when I eat all your meals for you," she agreed in a plaintive tone.

Annabel continued, distracted by her planning. "I shall leave this evening to ride overnight, so I reach his estate by midmorning."

"Overnight!" cried the housekeeper.

"Yes, there will be less chance of being seen. It is a full moon tonight, so I can see to ride."

"But blackguards ... and highwaymen ... and ... and men!"

"Mrs. Harris, I will ride steadily all night to save the horse's stamina, so I can ride like the wind if I hear so much as a twig snap. I will take the double-barrel pistol to protect myself. No one will expect to waylay a lone rider after midnight. Now let me see Mr. Gibbons to discuss which mount will traverse the distance best."

The normally cheerful matron croaked in despair as she dropped her head into her folded arms on the table. "Child, you will be the death of me."

"Felicitations on your birthday, Your Grace."

Philip Markham, the seventh Duke of Halmesbury, grimaced at his reflection in the mirror. "Thank you, Jones. I am afraid, however, that with the advent of my thirtieth birthday, it is time to attend to my duty. I shall have to brave the vapidness of the coming Season in search of a new wife."

"Indeed, Your Grace. It will be a pleasant change to have a lady in residence." Jones kept a straight face as Philip snorted.

"Only if the young lady cares to allow me to warm her heart," muttered Philip under his breath.

"Your Grace?"

"Nothing, Jones. Nothing worth repeating."

Shortly after Jones had left the room, Philip turned back to his reflection in the looking glass, its carved gilded frame a testament to generations of Markhams who had stood where he now stood. All this history, the family legacy he was duty-bound to protect for the next generation, weighed like a heavy mantle across his shoulders. It had not always felt like such a burden, but the events of the past few years had taken their toll. Now, at thirty years of age, he had been married and widowed, yet was childless. Somehow, this birthday did not feel like one to celebrate.

He squared his shoulders. Never mind that—it had been three long years since his wife's passing. It was time to move on. He could see faint lines forming at the corners of his eyes, mild furrows between his brows. He wished for smile lines to match, but there had been little in his life to smile about for some time.

His loneliness was a palpable pall that permeated the depths of his soul. *Palpable pall that permeated?* He groaned. It was regrettable to find himself waxing poetic, a sure sign it was high time to relinquish his hermitage. His lack of stimulating company was slowly driving him mad.

It had long been his dream to fill Halmesbury Manor with the sounds of children's laughter, to share love and warmth with his family by the time he reached this milestone birthday. His own parents had provided a happy, vibrant home when he was a boy. Yet time had crept forward, and here he was, alone—no wife, no children to carry on his name. Life had upended his plans in ways he could not have foreseen. His marriage to Jane Marley had been his first mistake. Bumbling their wedding night had set the tone for their strained relationship. His overzealous attentiveness had stifled her, and he had driven her to—

Philip forced himself to stop. No sense in dwelling on the past. That chapter was closed. He would learn from his mistakes and strive for better. His next bride would be bold, a woman of spirit who could share companionship and joy, not one who was timid or unwilling to communicate. Together, they could build a home filled with love and the children he had dreamed of for so long.

His parents' untimely deaths had left him yearning for the kind of family they had shared, one of connection and mutual affection. But his cousin Richard—he grimaced at the thought—had been a constant thorn in his side, a treacherous presence he was grateful to be rid of.

No matter. Richard no longer mattered. What mattered now was finding the right duchess. His own passions had cooled with time, and he no longer yearned for a romantic whirlwind. Instead, he sought a partnership of mutual respect and shared purpose. He would be pragmatic, not foolish. A pleasant, steady marriage with a strong, intelligent woman was not too much to hope for after years of reflection.

Philip inspected his reflection. His figure was still robust, his posture straight from years of riding and occasional brawls at his London club. His tailored navy coat, linen shirt, and buckskins fit impeccably. He reached to adjust a brass button on his waistcoat. Yes, he still cut a fine figure.

His future bride must be unconventional—a young woman unbroken by society's narrow expectations, someone with intelligence and vitality. He wanted a wife who could meet his gaze, speak her mind, and share a genuine connection.

He would not settle for timidity. He desired what his parents had—a marriage of equals filled with mutual understanding. With renewed resolve, he turned from the mirror.

For my birthday, I give myself permission to seek a bride and plan for the next generation of Markhams.

∽

ANNABEL'S back and thighs were aching by the time she rode up to a copse of trees bordering the front drive of Avonmead. She had ridden through the night, and she estimated it was now about ten o'clock in the morning.

As she gazed up at the impressive Palladian edifice rising two towering stories, she felt her pulse quicken with trepidation. Should she walk up one of the front stone staircases to the portico and simply knock on the hardwood doors? Surely the servants would not grant her entry based on her unconventional attire. If they turned her away, the enormous risk she took in traveling here would be for naught. Why had she not brought a change of clothes? She'd been so focused on the journey, she had not thought ahead to the arrival. She could have cleaned up at the lake she had seen in the distance and donned a walking dress and pelisse to present herself at the front door as a lady. As she was now, she would appear to be a lout, if she even fooled the attending servant into thinking she was a lad in such proximity.

She sighed in resignation. It was too late to regret her lack of preparation now. Her nerves were starting to fail her. Hopefully, he was not one of those peers who slept half the day away. She was counting on him being an industrious man, as the magazine suggested, who rose early. If not, it would force her to hide out somewhere until he made an appearance.

Tick-tock, Annabel, tick-tock.

With the reminder of her impending wedding day racing toward her, she steeled her nerves and dismounted, tying Starling to one of the sturdy lower branches.

She rolled her shoulders to stretch out. The bulky overcoat had grown uncomfortable within the last couple of hours of riding. She was grateful that her expedition was occurring mid-autumn, as the overcoat was a necessary part of her disguise. A month or two earlier, it would have been far too warm to have kept the coat on for the duration. As it was, she warmed to an uncomfortable degree after dawn had broken across the eastern sky to herald the start of the day. Right about the time she entered Wiltshire County, when the air had sounded with birdcalls as if to welcome her arrival.

Her ride had been uneventful, having started out from Baydon Hall at midnight with the full moon lighting a brilliant path on the roadways to be navigated. She concealed herself only twice in the woods and hedges to the side of the roads when oncoming mail coaches neared her position.

Swiping her brow and neck with a handkerchief, she considered her quest. The Duke of Halmesbury was her last chance to change her fate. If the quest failed, she would have to do something truly desperate to outwit her father's plans, not to mention Richard's despicable ideals of perfect marriage.

She may not be a beautiful English rose, but she must value herself, just as Mama had always instructed. Annabel's only hope was to receive a warm reception rather than find herself in worsening circumstances. She prayed this was not a matter of leaping from the frying pan into the fire. The duke's reputation was excellent, but she did not know what sort of man he really was. A kind one, she hoped with fervor.

Now that a plan was in motion, instead of lamenting her circumstances between arguments with her father, Annabel felt the fire of determination fueling her forward. Her body might tremble with exhaustion, but that fire would continue to energize her through this struggle. She must see this through, and she must succeed. Considering the walk up the driveway, she noted the leafy bushes would shield her from the manor windows.

She rubbed the gelding's ears.

"Good boy, Starling. Thank you for getting me here safely," she whispered in a warm voice, feeding him a carrot from her coat pocket. With a pat, she turned and quickly started across the drive toward the bushes, stooping to remain hidden as long as possible as she tried to think how to proceed. Once she reached the majestic stone structure, she would find a way to talk to the duke. He would be in residence, and he would agree to help her.

Fortune favors the bold, Annabel.

She climbed the stone steps on the left to reach the massive oak doors. The house boasted two symmetrical staircases converging onto a colonnaded portico, she noted, her mind wandering onto vague topics as her courage failed. Forcing herself forward, she stood in front of the doors and tentatively used the brass knocker.

No one came to the door.

She surmised the servants may be occupied in other parts of the house, not expecting a visit so much earlier than conventional visiting times. Bravado and caution warred, a dichotomy within her mind as she tried to work out how to proceed until a single thought, voiced in her mother's clear tones, whispered.

Sometimes, discretion is the better part of valor.

Perhaps she did not need to convince the servants to allow her entry. This was a country estate quite a distance from the local village and, if this household was anything like Baydon Hall, there was a chance that the front door was not locked while the servants went about their early morning errands. Ignoring her deafening heartbeats, the thumping so loud it surely could be heard all the way back to Baydon Hall, she saw her hand reach for the handle as if it had a mind of its own. Her choice was apparently made—if the door was unlocked, she was going to walk into the manor and find the duke.

If, heaven forfend, she was caught, the servants would be compelled to report her intrusion and grant her an audience with the master of the house.

CHAPTER
TWO

"The world was to me a secret which I desired to divine."

Mary Shelley's Frankenstein

∽

P hilip was seated at his desk, the polished mahogany surface gleaming in the midmorning light. A soft breeze stirred the papers before him, drifting in through the open window. With the unseasonal warmth, he had propped the study door ajar to allow air to circulate. He hated working in stifling rooms. As he reviewed the figures spread across his desk, he sensed, rather than saw, that he was being watched.

"Clinton?" he called, setting down his quill. When no answer came, he glanced up, expecting his butler. Instead, his gaze landed on a young lad standing hesitantly just inside the doorway, dressed like a stable hand. Philip frowned. "Who are you?" he asked sharply.

The lad stepped into the room, his movements nervous

yet determined. He walked straight to the chairs positioned before Philip's desk and stopped, hands clenched at his sides. "Your Grace," the boy said in a hoarse whisper.

"I said, who are you? And what are you doing in my study?" Philip's frown deepened. "You are not one of my stable lads."

"You recognize all your stable lads?" the boy countered.

"Indeed, I do. Now, explain yourself before I call Clinton to have you removed."

"I have come from Filminster to seek your assistance," the boy said, voice trembling yet resolute.

Philip leaned forward, suspicion narrowing his gaze. Something about the boy's tone seemed ... off. And that bulky coat—why wear such a thing in this balmy weather? He opened his mouth to demand an explanation, but the boy cleared his throat and spoke again. This time, the pitch of his voice rose higher, carrying a distinctly feminine quality.

Philip blinked. Could it be ... a girl?

The boy—or rather, the girl—confirmed his suspicions by removing her hat and shrugging off the oversized coat. Before him stood a slender figure dressed in buckskin breeches and a billowing linen shirt. The curve of her hips and the faint outline of her bosom left no doubt. He sat back in his chair, startled. "What is this?" he demanded, dragging his gaze from her figure to her face.

"I came from Filminster to seek your help," she said, her voice steady despite her apparent nervousness. "You are my last resort."

Philip stared, his mind working furiously to make sense of this unexpected visitor. The girl was young, well-spoken, and clearly determined. Her chestnut hair, neatly plaited, framed a face that was earnest and intelligent. Whoever she was, she had gone to great lengths to reach him.

"Desperate enough to ride all this way, dressed as a boy?" he asked, his voice laced with incredulity.

"Yes," she replied simply. "I would have done more if necessary."

"More?"

"More ... such as sell all my jewels and run off to Scotland." She gazed out the window, clearly imagining a lengthy journey in her mind rather than the gardens her eyes appeared to be focused on.

He studied her for a moment, taking in the determined glint as she returned her gaze to meet his, leaving no doubt that she would do such a thing.

"Scotland." Philip raised a brow at her boldness. "And you are ...?"

"Miss Annabel Ridley, daughter of Lord Josiah Ridley, Baron of Filminster," she said, curtsying awkwardly in her breeches. "Pleased to make your acquaintance, Your Grace."

The name sparked a memory. Philip tilted his head. "Filminster? That means ... are you betrothed to my cousin, Richard Balfour?"

Her lips tightened at the mention of her fiancé. "Quite. I am to wed Lord Saunton, and that is why I need your help ... to break the betrothal."

Philip stared at her, stunned. Of all the reasons a young lady might barge into his study in disguise, this was not one he had anticipated. "You rode all night to reach me?"

"Yes," she said, gesturing to her attire. "I had my housekeeper cover for me by pretending I was unwell. No one will visit me in my rooms if I am ill, and I rode through the night to reach Avonmead. It is a beautiful park."

Philip rubbed his temples. "Miss Ridley, that was an

incredibly dangerous journey. You could have been harmed."

Her chin lifted. "It was necessary. My future is at stake."

He studied her for a long moment, impressed by the fire in her eyes. She was no timid debutante, that much was certain. "And what makes you think I can help?"

"You are a man of influence, Your Grace," she replied. "The articles about your charitable works suggested you were a fair and just man. I believed you might listen to my plight and offer guidance."

Philip sighed and gestured toward the sofa near the window. "Please, sit down. It seems you have much to tell me."

As she crossed the room, Philip closed the study door, ensuring their conversation remained private. He returned to his seat, watching her closely. This young woman had taken an extraordinary risk to reach him. Her boldness was both concerning and intriguing.

Could she be the solution to his own predicament? The thought was absurd ... and yet, not entirely unwelcome. For now, he set it aside, choosing instead to listen to her story. If nothing else, this encounter would be far more engaging than the dreary rounds of social calls that awaited him this coming Season.

∼

ANNABEL ADMIRED the splendid Chippendale sofa positioned below the window, its rich upholstery framed perfectly by a crimson Anatolian rug. As inviting as it looked, she hesitated to sit, mindful of her sweat-dampened clothes. Instead, she moved to a mahogany armchair near the sofa and sank into it with a sigh of relief. Her legs ached from the long ride, and she shifted slightly, trying to ease the discomfort while maintaining an air of confidence.

As the duke approached and settled onto the sofa, she could not help but notice his striking appearance. The sunlight streaming through the window caught his blond hair, turning it to spun gold. He was tall, well over six feet, with broad shoulders and a commanding presence. His strong jaw, straight nose, and thick blond eyebrows gave him an air of effortless authority. He looked like he had stepped from the pages of an illustrated history of Viking chieftains.

The sheer vitality of the man was unlike anything Annabel had encountered. Where Richard's charm had always seemed polished and practiced, the Duke of Halmesbury exuded natural strength and composure. It was disconcerting, to say the least, and she fought to regain her focus.

Pull yourself together, Annabel.

The duke leaned back comfortably, his gray eyes sharp yet not unkind. "Would you like to start at the beginning, Miss Ridley? Why have you sought me out?"

Annabel met his gaze and congratulated herself on having come this far. Now, she only needed to summon the courage to speak her truth. "I have known Richard for a long time," she began. "He is a boyhood friend of my brother, Brendan, and Saunton Park is near my home, Baydon Hall. Over the years, he has been something of a confidant. I ... I do not have many friends."

She glanced down, twisting her fingers together in her lap. "My father does not like to leave the estate unless necessary, and he rarely allows me to travel. Unless my aunt visits, and then only when she chaperones me to Filminster events."

The duke's expression softened. "Your mother is not present?"

Annabel's lips curved into a wistful smile. "No. She passed away nearly eleven years ago. Mama was wonderful. If she were here, I would not need to trouble you. She would never have allowed things to progress this far."

The duke inclined his head slightly. "And what has happened?"

Annabel took a steadying breath. "I thought I knew Richard. He was kind when my father was not, and when Brendan ..." Her voice faltered. "When Brendan lost interest in me, I craved the attention and I imagined myself in love with him. When he proposed, I was overjoyed. It seemed like a chance to escape my father's criticisms and restrictions. But ..."

She hesitated, heat flooding her cheeks. "I was naïve. Richard made me feel special, but I now see how blind I was. A month ago, I ... I discovered him behaving inappropriately with our kitchen maid in the stables."

The duke inhaled sharply, sitting straighter. He folded his arms across his chest and exhaled slowly, as though reining in his emotions. Annabel felt a rush of relief. At last, someone recognized the wrongness of what she had endured.

He lowered his arms and leaned forward, resting his hands on his knees. "I am very sorry you were exposed to Richard's indiscretions in such a crude manner. I know him to be a rake, but I had hoped he possessed some sense of delicacy."

Annabel managed a small, grateful smile. "It is such a relief to speak with someone who understands my predicament."

His brow furrowed slightly. "You mean to say others do not?"

She nodded sadly. "When I confronted Richard, he dismissed my concerns and declared the wedding would proceed. My father was equally unyielding. He believes Richard is the best match I could hope for, and he says such behavior is typical among men of Richard's station. My brother is in London, and I have not spoken with him in years. My aunt will not even entertain a discussion about the matter."

The duke grimaced. "And yet you feel strongly that the marriage should not proceed."

Annabel straightened, her chin lifting slightly. "I want a proper marriage with an honorable man. If love is not possible, then at least warmth and mutual respect. I wish for a family—a faithful husband and children to cherish. Richard's deceitful nature makes any of that impossible." Her voice trembled with conviction. "I would rather have an honest marriage of convenience with shared goals than endure this farce."

~

Philip leaned back slightly, regarding Miss Ridley with a mixture of admiration and intrigue. "I see your point. I value integrity myself."

Miss Ridley's expression softened in relief.

"You rode a long way to find me," he continued. "I assume you have a solution in mind. What exactly are you asking me to do for you?"

"I was hoping you would speak to Richard. He has always spoken of you with reverence. Perhaps you could convince him to release me from the betrothal?"

Philip considered her words. A beautiful, intelligent woman, bold enough to seize control of her future, had come directly to him for aid. She was striking, self-possessed, and everything he had wished for during his musings that very morning. Unlike the timid young women he had encountered in the past, Miss Ridley had a passion and vitality that drew his attention.

The opportunity she presented was undeniable. Helping her avoid a marriage to Richard—an irredeemable rogue, in Philip's estimation—could also solve his own problem. He needed a wife, and Annabel Ridley possessed the spirit, intelligence, and strength he valued. This was not mere fortune; this was the recognition of an opportunity and acting upon it.

Mind made up, he declared, "I agree to help."

She blinked, clearly shocked, before her brandy-colored eyes lit with joy. "You will speak to Richard?"

Philip's chest tightened at her effervescent smile, but he focused on the matter at hand. "Unfortunately, my cousin and I are no longer in contact. We have not spoken in three years, which is why you and I have not had the pleasure of meeting before today. However," he added, leaning forward slightly, "I have a much better plan."

Annabel's brow furrowed. "A better plan?"

Philip nodded, choosing his words carefully.

"A plan my cousin cannot fight." He hesitated briefly, gathering his resolve. *Fortune favors the bold, Philip.* "I will marry you instead."

Annabel's mouth fell open in astonishment. "What?"

"You need a husband who can rival Richard's social standing," Philip explained, his tone steady and matter-of-fact. "Your father would likely be overjoyed to secure a connection to a duke rather than an earl. As for myself, I need a wife. You strike me as intelligent and determined—qualities I admire. I believe we could have a successful partnership."

Annabel's cheeks flushed as her gaze faltered. "You would engage in a marriage of convenience? With me?"

"Yes. A marriage built on mutual respect and shared goals is superior to many marriages I know. It would certainly be preferable to my first marriage."

Her brow creased with uncertainty. "But why me? Why would you do this for me?"

Philip held her gaze for a moment, willing himself to remain composed. He could confess that her boldness impressed him, or that he found her far more intriguing than any woman he had met in years. He could even admit to the relief of avoiding another Season filled with idle conversations and tedious introductions. But he settled on a simpler answer.

"It is the gentlemanly thing to do," he said with a faint smile. "I would be honored to assist you in resolving this matter."

Her shoulders relaxed slightly, though her expression remained wary. "You would marry me without love?"

Philip inclined his head. "Love is not something I seek. What I value is companionship, respect, and shared purpose. I believe we could offer that to each other. You are a bold, capable young woman, and I believe you would make an excellent wife."

Annabel bit her lip, her uncertainty evident. Philip gave her a moment to process his offer. He needed to handle this carefully if he was to win her agreement.

"Consider the advantages," he continued. "You would no longer be under your father's control or subject to Richard's whims. You would have independence within a household that values your voice and your choices. And you would gain the security of a partnership with someone who respects you."

Annabel studied him intently, her brandy eyes searching his face for sincerity. At last, she nodded slightly, as if coming to terms with the possibility. "You have given me much to think about, Your Grace."

Philip allowed himself a small smile. "That is all I ask, Miss Ridley. Think on it. We can discuss the matter further while I give you a tour of Avonmead."

As she inclined her head in agreement, Philip felt a flicker of hope. This arrangement, unexpected as it was, held the promise of a future far more fulfilling than anything he had anticipated that morning.

∽

After her initial surprise waned, Annabel allowed herself to consider the duke's offer. The options remaining to her were scarce, so the decision did not take long—barely a few seconds.

Her gaze shifted to him, a man renowned for his honor and integrity. He was, she admitted to herself, pleasing to look at. A faithful marriage to a handsome duke, founded on honesty and shared goals, was far better than the disastrous future she had been fighting to avoid. Still, doubts tugged at the edges of her thoughts. She had never envisioned herself as a duchess. Was she prepared for such a role?

Her situation had felt like a tightening noose, the future already planned for her. Yet here, almost at the very hour of her metaphorical execution, was an unexpected reprieve. The Duke of Halmesbury offered not just escape, but the chance for a promising future. Decisiveness was key now—she had to act swiftly. Surely, she would be a fool to reject the opportunity before her? Women of the *ton* vied for such matches; how many noblemen of his rank, charm, and appearance would offer marriage on sight? If any.

Her mother's voice seemed to echo in her mind, full of approval. This was an improved outcome, the sort of chance Mama would have urged her to seize.

Besides, what if she hesitated, and he changed his mind? The duke might realize she had little to offer him and withdraw the proposal. Better to secure the promise now, before he reconsidered.

As her thoughts raced, she became aware of his steady, patient gaze. The duke's composure put her at ease, even as her pulse quickened. She liked this man. He seemed approachable, kind, and grounded—qualities she admired. And he was one of the most attractive man she had ever encountered. Could she marry him?

It struck her then: they did not truly know each other. But had she not known Richard for nearly a decade? Yet she had not known him at all. *The Stable Incident* had proven that time spent in someone's company was no guarantee of understanding their character. This decision, Annabel realized, would rest not on time, but on instinct.

But look where your instincts have gotten you before, a voice inside her warned.

That was true—but it was also not the whole truth. She was no longer the woman she had been a month ago. Discovering Richard's betrayal had been a pivotal moment, reshaping her perspective. She had spent the past weeks reflecting deeply on life, character, and integrity. The poetry and philosophy she had read over the years had taken on new meaning, teaching her the true nature of love, trust, and betrayal.

She might not be a great beauty or a celebrated social success, but she believed in her own worth. She had the right to pursue happiness, just like anyone else.

What truly mattered now was whether she trusted her ability to appraise the man before her. Did her instincts tell her he was someone she could trust? And if they did, was she brave enough to take the leap of faith?

Meeting his gaze, she found herself smiling. "Perhaps you could show me your home and tell me about what marriage with you would be like?" she ventured.

The duke's grin in response was both warm and genuine, lighting his features in a way that made her pulse flutter. "What a splendid idea," he said.

Annabel blinked, momentarily caught off guard by how his full, sculpted lips revealed perfect white teeth against sun-bronzed skin. He was, undeniably, exceptional to behold—even more so when he smiled.

CHAPTER
THREE

"I am content to reason with you."

Mary Shelley's Frankenstein

~

"Before we proceed, have you eaten anything today?" Halmesbury asked.

Annabel couldn't help the smile that spread across her face, but she quickly tempered it. His solicitousness was appealing, but she reminded herself not to judge too hastily. Richard had often appeared solicitous, only to use it as a tool for manipulation. Kindness could not be taken at face value; it needed time and consistency to prove its authenticity. If she accepted this man's offer of marriage, she would be entrusting him with her future—there would be no undoing such a decision.

"I have not," she admitted. "I am, in truth, famished."

"Very well. I will have a light meal prepared," the duke

replied. He paused, then added, "Mrs. Thorne—I mean, Clinton—will see to it."

"Mrs. Thorne?"

"Mrs. Thorne was my housekeeper until recently. She approached me with concerns about the poor conditions at the Halmesbury Home for Children. Together, we worked to improve the facility, which has since been renamed the Halmesbury Home for Beloved Children. Mrs. Thorne is now its matron. She is an extraordinary woman—competent and compassionate. The children are fortunate to have her care and attention." His tone softened with genuine respect. "As for us, we are managing without her, though not without difficulty. Clinton has taken on additional responsibilities with the assistance of a senior maid. My wife"—he coughed lightly—"if I had one, would be involved in sorting it out."

Annabel grinned. "That is shameless."

The duke arched a golden eyebrow. "I do not know to what you are referring."

"You are using your admirable philanthropic efforts as a bribe to sway me, along with the promise of managing this elegant home."

Halmesbury shrugged, his expression entirely unrepentant, as he rang for Clinton and returned to his seat on the red-and-ivory striped Chippendale sofa. Annabel could not help but notice the way his broad shoulders filled his navy coat. His posture was relaxed, his manner at ease, suggesting he did not stand on formality within his private domain.

There was a knock at the door.

"Enter," Halmesbury called.

An elderly butler stepped inside. Tall and slim, with a

distinguished air and graying hair, he glanced briefly at Annabel before addressing the duke.

"Miss Ridley and I would care for a light meal," Halmesbury said. "Perhaps tea and sandwiches. Please see it is prepared quickly."

Clinton bowed.

"And," the duke added, "Miss Ridley's presence here is not public knowledge. Ensure the servants understand this visit is not to be discussed."

"Of course, Your Grace," Clinton rasped in a hoarse voice. He bowed again and turned to leave.

"Oh, and Clinton," Halmesbury lifted a brow to Annabel in question. "Miss Ridley has a mount we should see to?"

Annabel nodded. "Starling is tied to the first copse of trees near the drive, just beyond the bushes."

Clinton nodded. "I will send a groomsman to retrieve the mount, Miss Ridley." With a final bow, he exited the study, closing the door softly behind him.

"So, Miss Ridley," Halmesbury said, turning his attention back to her, "do you have any questions while we wait for your meal?"

Annabel hesitated briefly, then said, "What would make you a better choice than Lord Saunton?"

"For one, I am committed to being faithful to my wife. I believe that was an important criterion?"

Annabel nodded.

"And, like you, I wish to build a family and enjoy a harmonious household. I would not leave you isolated at my country estate, which I suspect is what Lord Saunton had planned. When I go to London, I would want you at my side, sharing in the duties and social commitments. That said, I prefer life here at Avonmead, so we would spend much of our time at home. Together."

"That sounds promising," Annabel admitted.

Halmesbury smiled. "I am also invested in the well-being of my tenants and the community. I am currently improving the tenant homes, expanding the local school, and establishing a vocational program for the older children at the Halmesbury Home. I would welcome a wife who could assist with these projects, as well as manage the household."

"I would love to be involved," Annabel replied earnestly. "I have always visited our tenants and tried to help where my father allowed. Sometimes a little more than he permitted, if I am being honest." She smiled wryly. "What the baron does not know cannot be criticized."

The duke chuckled softly. "Good. I will be honest in return—I do want children."

"Of course," Annabel said, inclining her head.

Halmesbury hesitated briefly, as though choosing his next words carefully. "And I do intend to engage in the activities that lead to children."

Annabel swallowed hard, heat rising to her cheeks. She knew little of what those activities entailed, though she had a vague understanding. The candid way he spoke surprised her, though it also reassured her of his honesty. She could imagine that intimacy with a man like Halmesbury would be ... agreeable.

She quickly banished the thought and managed a composed smile. "That sounds agreeable to me."

For the briefest moment, a look of relief flickered across Halmesbury's face before he returned to his usual calm demeanor. Annabel could not help but wonder what had passed through his mind, though she supposed she might find out in time.

They lingered over their impromptu meal, their conversation flowing easily as the duke spoke of his estate and tenants. He described the improvements he had implemented over the years with a balance of passion and practicality. Annabel listened intently, impressed by his dedication. His plans were carefully designed to benefit both the estate's profitability and the well-being of his tenants.

It was clear to her Halmesbury viewed himself as a caretaker, striving to create equilibrium within his community. He introduced changes gradually, ensuring they would be sustainable and harmonious. His attention to both the broader vision and the finer details revealed a thoughtful leader. To Annabel, this only heightened his appeal as a potential husband.

"I make the decisions regarding the stables at Baydon Hall," Annabel offered, encouraged by his openness. "With my brother gone these past four years and my father rarely involved, I have worked closely with our stable master to maintain them. It is one area where I have had some autonomy."

She paused mid-sentence as their hands brushed while reaching for the same sandwich. The touch of his warm fingers sent an unexpected tingle up her arm, and she quickly withdrew her hand, willing herself to maintain composure.

"Please, go ahead," he said, his voice courteous as he gestured for her to take the sandwich.

Annabel hesitated, wishing—though she dared not admit it aloud—that he had left his hand resting on hers. Richard had often touched her in passing over the years, but his touch had never elicited such a reaction. She began to see her relationship with Richard for what it truly was: a comfortable familiarity, not the grand love she had once naively believed.

"How many mounts do you have at Baydon Hall?" the duke asked, smoothly steering the conversation forward.

As Annabel answered, she acknowledged to herself how intoxicating it was to have his full attention. He listened with genuine interest, his engaging manner putting her at ease. She quelled any inclination to flirt, determined to match his calm and composed manner.

Once their meal concluded, Halmesbury led her on a tour of the house. The grand library captivated her immediately. Its soaring bookcases, shaped arches, and a large medallion inset against towering windows overlooking the parkland gave the room a majestic air with the added whimsy of Moroccan influences. Annabel felt a pang of longing to explore its shelves at leisure. The thought of having access to such a collection was yet another reason to seriously consider his proposal.

They moved on to the portrait gallery, where a long line of family portraits stretched along the right wall, interspersed with Italian marble sculptures and tall windows on the left. Halmesbury guided her down the gallery, sharing stories of seven generations of the Markham family.

"... and this was my mother," he said, stopping before the portrait of a serene, elegant woman. "She passed away when I was a boy, during childbirth. She loved lively debates and brought a sense of unity to our family. I miss the feeling of togetherness she created."

"I am sorry for your loss," Annabel said gently. "And your father?"

"He died a few years after my mother," Halmesbury

replied. "I suspect he never recovered from losing her. Without her to anchor us, our family slowly drifted apart. My younger brother, Sebastian, is currently on his Grand Tour. He writes occasionally but has been away for some time." He paused, then added, "But I miss having family here. This house can feel empty without them."

Annabel nodded, sensing his loneliness.

As they approached the next portrait, the duke's expression shifted. The painting depicted a beautiful woman with golden curls and crystalline blue eyes, dressed in elegant court attire. Halmesbury's jaw tightened as he averted his gaze, looking toward the far end of the gallery as though seeking an escape.

"This is my late wife, Jane," he said finally, his voice subdued.

Annabel remained silent, allowing him the space to continue. The air between them felt heavy, thick with unspoken emotions. It was clear he had loved his wife deeply, and Annabel felt a pang of something she could not name.

"She was a proper daughter of polite society," Halmesbury said, his tone measured. "But we were not well-matched. I regret not taking the time to truly know her before we wed. Our marriage was strained before she fell ill."

Annabel gazed at the portrait, marveling at the late duchess's flawless beauty. Encased in a gilded frame, Jane held a place of honor in the gallery. Annabel could easily imagine what had first attracted the duke to her. Compared to such perfection, she felt acutely aware of her own disheveled state: her sweat-dampened buckskins, limp linen shirt, and hair in a simple plait.

What could he possibly desire from her?

Seize the day, Annabel, she told herself firmly. *Not tear yourself to pieces.* Squaring her shoulders, she resolved to focus on what truly mattered: the man before her and the possibilities of their future.

∼

Philip stared up at the face of his late wife. He rarely ventured into the portrait gallery, avoiding this particular image that reminded him of an unhappy time. Yet today, he felt compelled to confront it. Annabel deserved honesty about his past—about his imperfections. She needed to know he had experienced failure in the most personal of unions.

He had not realized, until those early days of his first marriage, that he could be selfish. Jane had been young and shy, her delicate nature unsuited to the strength of his personality. Her silences, her tears, and her eventual retreat into isolation had revealed truths about himself that he could not ignore. Somehow, without meaning to, he had driven her to despair.

Her ghost lingered in his thoughts. The knowledge that he had failed her haunted him, even now. He had lacked sufficient patience, gentleness, and understanding. The realization had come too late to undo the damage. Her death had cemented his regrets, leaving him to grapple with the consequences of his self-absorption.

But those regrets had also taught him valuable lessons. He had learned from his mistakes and resolved to do better. He could not remain in solitude forever, locked in a half-life of regret. His thirtieth birthday had dawned with the startling awareness that three years had passed while he merely existed, not truly living.

It was time to try again.

Annabel was nothing like Jane. Where his late wife had been quiet and retiring, Annabel was bold, fiery, and untamed. Her strength was a magnet for his own, drawing him toward a possibility he had not dared imagine. If he approached their union with care, he believed he could build something real, something lasting, with this remarkable woman.

The thought gave him hope.

"My late wife was a restrained and proper daughter of polite society," he continued, his voice steady though his heart felt exposed.

He glanced at Annabel, gauging her reaction. She listened intently, her expression unreadable but not dismissive. Encouraged, he continued.

"I am afraid I did not get to know her as well as I would have wished before she passed. Our brief marriage was ... strained, even before she fell ill. There are things I wish I had done differently, lessons I have taken to heart."

He let the admission settle between them, the weight of his words filling the quiet. As he looked back at Jane's portrait, he made a silent vow:

I will not repeat my mistakes. I will treat Annabel with care. I will not overwhelm her with my ardor or let my impatience push her away. If she will have me, I will protect her, cherish her, and honor her as I failed to do with Jane.

Closing his eyes briefly, he steadied himself. When he turned to Annabel, he found her watching him closely. Her thoughtful gaze unsettled him. What was she thinking?

Was she repulsed by his past? By the admission of his flaws and the weight of his history? He could not blame her if she was. But the thought of losing her—of her choosing to walk away—clenched his chest in a way he had not expected.

He valued her presence more than he could articulate. She was vibrant and compelling, her intelligence and wit a match for his own. In the short time they had spent together, she had stirred feelings he had thought dormant. He hoped, fervently, that he had not scared her away with his candor.

Pretending patience he did not feel, Philip returned her gaze, waiting for her response.

∽

As Annabel stood in silence, she realized it would be difficult, if not impossible, to compete with the late duchess in the duke's heart. It was clear how deeply his feelings ran. Halmesbury was not a demonstrative man, but beneath his composed exterior, he felt things with a depth that set him apart from any other man she had ever known.

Earlier, he had spoken of his estate and his responsibilities with a passion that revealed his care for others. He was a man of genuine emotion and honor, and her heart wanted to trust him.

She wanted this. She wanted it far more than a lifetime tied to faithless Richard.

Annabel turned her gaze back to the painting. The duchess was riveting—her soft blonde curls, crystal blue eyes, and poised elegance were the epitome of perfection. In comparison, Annabel felt all too aware of her own perceived shortcomings. Her father had never hesitated to point out her unfashionable olive skin, her darker hair, and the figure that defied conventional ideals: hips a bit too rounded, a frame a bit too slim, and a bosom a bit too full.

"She was a beautiful woman," Annabel murmured.

"Yes," Halmesbury replied simply. "The duchess was a diamond of the first water."

Annabel glanced down at her masculine attire, her buckskins and linen shirt clinging after her long ride. Standing before the portrait of such a refined lady, she felt like a world apart. She could imagine Jane excelling at all the ladylike pursuits that had eluded her own interest—playing the pianoforte, needlework, singing. Annabel had never mastered any of it.

It was as if it were a before-and-after comparison perhaps, with Annabel representing the *before*. *Before* attending finishing school, *before* an introduction to court, and *before* visiting a London modiste for an appropriate wardrobe.

"I must be honest," she admitted, her voice quiet. "I would have much to learn to become a proper duchess."

Halmesbury's tone was reassuring. "We will hire a companion and tutors to prepare you."

She nodded, though the comparison to Jane lingered. Unlike the late duchess, Annabel had not captivated this man across a ballroom or inspired a romantic pursuit. He had not sought her out, compelled by some irresistible force. No, she had fallen into his lap at precisely the moment when, for reasons she did not fully understand, she met his private criteria for a wife.

Perhaps the only thing in her favor was her timing, and that Halmesbury felt inclined to help her. She knew he could find a wife who was more gracious, more beautiful, and more deserving of his attentions.

"The *ton* will not be kind when they compare me to her," she declared softly.

Halmesbury snorted. "As a collective, the *ton* is never

kind. But you are an original, Miss Ridley. And as my wife, no one I care about will dare to be unkind."

Annabel felt a warmth bloom in her chest at his words. She was unused to such appreciation, and his compliment made her feel unique, even beautiful. Whatever had prompted the duke's offer, today she allowed herself a moment of selfishness. This was her chance to change her fate.

No longer would she have to risk a perilous journey to Scotland, relying only on her mother's jewels to survive. She could marry the duke. And, if she were honest with herself, she wanted to know this fascinating man of hidden depths. He was a man who treated others with dignity and kindness, even when there was nothing for him to gain. It had been so long since anyone had truly cared for her—not since Mama.

"Thank you, Your Grace," she said, her voice steady despite the emotions swirling within her.

Annabel knew, as surely as she had known in the stable a month ago, that this moment would change her life forever. She did not know what the future held, but she understood the gravity of the decision before her.

For weeks, she had felt like a leaf in the wind, carried wherever her father's ambitions and Richard's indifference dictated. Now, for the first time in weeks, someone had offered her a choice.

She could walk away and accept the future her father had arranged—a future of neglect and isolation at Richard's country seat. Or she could take a chance on this man, this guarded but generous stranger, who promised to stand by her side.

Her pulse quickened as her thoughts came into focus.

Fortune favors the bold, Annabel.

"I accept."

The words hung in the air, decisive and clear. Her heart pounded in her chest, but her resolve held firm.

Annabel looked at Halmesbury, the guarded man who had offered her a lifeline, and felt a flicker of hope. She liked him—more than liked him. She respected him. And she would do everything in her power to make this unexpected partnership not only work, but thrive.

CHAPTER
FOUR

"There is something at work in my soul which I do not understand."

Mary Shelley's Frankenstein

∽

Philip smiled, working to contain his delight. Every instinct told him this was right. This was no mere coincidence—it was destiny. An amazing quirk of fate had placed Annabel Ridley on his path, and he knew, without doubt, that this day would redefine his future.

This girl was special. This moment was special. It felt as though the very hands of providence were altering the course of his life.

And Richard is going to be furious. That thought brought an added rush of satisfaction, mixing triumph with his joy.

Philip was careful to hide the flood of emotions coursing through him, keeping his demeanor steady even as his heart raced with excitement.

"Excellent," he said warmly, taking her hand in his. He raised it to his lips and pressed a kiss to her gloved fingers, his touch lingering just a moment longer than propriety dictated. "Our partnership shall be long and happy, my dear Miss Ridley."

His mind filled with hopeful visions. He wanted a home filled with warmth, laughter, and life. He wanted to discover all the little things that made Annabel so fascinating, from her boldness to her quick wit. What books did she read? What dreams did she hold in her heart? What drove her to defy convention and ride through the night to seek him out?

He silently thanked his decision to agree to that magazine piece—an effort he had dismissed at the time as a silly vanity project. Yet it had drawn this extraordinary woman to him, and for that, he would be forever grateful.

He wanted to debate her ideas over dinner, share quiet moments in the library, and learn everything about her. She intrigued him like no one else ever had.

But now was not the time to indulge his dreams. He composed himself and spoke evenly. "I imagine you are in need of some rest after your journey. I will arrange for Clinton to find you something to wear while your riding clothes are cleaned. We can have dinner this evening, and tomorrow at first light, we will set out. I will see you safely home before your father has any reason to suspect your absence."

Annabel tilted her head, studying him. "You do not plan to tell him about my ... unconventional journey?"

Philip chuckled, shaking his head. "My dear Miss Ridley, I would not dare."

Relief bloomed across her face, her smile lighting up the

room. It was clear she had feared a reprimand, but instead, she had found an ally.

"As long as you promise," he added, "that you will not risk your lovely neck on any more dangerous, cross-country escapades."

Her eyes sparkled mischievously. "We shall see," she replied, her voice light with insolence. "Once you come up to scratch, I will consider your request."

Philip laughed heartily as he led her back into the hall. "Don't worry, Miss Ridley. We shall wed before the week is done. Until that happy moment, I shall not sleep a wink, for I must ensure Scotland plays no part in your future plans."

∽

Within half an hour, a tall, redheaded maid led Annabel into a grand, ornate bedchamber overlooking the gardens and woods behind the manor. Through the large sash windows, she could see far into the distance, a stunning tapestry of walled gardens, trees, and bushes in a riot of colors, dissecting the expansive lawns. A gleam of water beyond the trees hinted at a hidden lake.

She sighed in delight. The park was magnificent.

Annabel arrived at the chamber slightly breathless from the effort it had taken to reach it. Avonmead was vast, its two enormous wings stretching in either direction. The trek up a grand staircase with ornate balustrades and through several lengthy passages, combined with her earlier exploration of the estate alongside the duke, had demonstrated the mansion's immense size and scope.

The maid, however, showed no signs of weariness, her steady pace suggesting she was well accustomed to traversing such distances in her daily duties.

On the sky-blue jacquard counterpane, a fresh chemise had been laid out. Annabel's fingers brushed the fine fabric of the bedcovers, admiring the intricate damask pattern woven with glossy and matte threads. If this was the luxury of a guest chamber, the Markham family's private quarters must be astonishing.

Mary, the maid, cleared her throat. "I will help you undress to bathe, miss. We will have your ... riding clothes cleaned for the morning, and I will return to help you dress for dinner at about six this evening. His Grace instructed that you not be disturbed until then. We will find suitable garments for you to dine in."

Mary hesitated over the mention of Annabel's attire, and her disconcerted expression as she helped remove the unconventional clothing made it clear she was unsure what to make of it. Annabel suppressed a wry smile. No doubt, the girl had never encountered a woman daring enough to don masculine attire, and it left her feeling a bit self-conscious.

At Baydon Hall, the servants were tolerant of her eccentricities, but Annabel knew well that in more formal households, propriety was enforced with even greater rigor than among the peers they served. Richard had often regaled her with tales of his youthful exploits in such homes, though hindsight now made her wince. It was all too likely those anecdotes had omitted the disreputable details that caused the real trouble. Zooks, she had been naïve not to have questioned them more deeply!

A hand-painted screen of flowers and birds shielded the hammered copper tub positioned near the fireplace. Rising steam curled around its edges, and Mary's damp skin and slightly limp red hair attested to the effort she had expended filling it. Gathering Annabel's unconventional attire with visible discomfort, the maid made for the door.

"Thank you, Mary," Annabel said warmly.

The maid glanced back, her blue eyes rounding as if startled. Annabel supposed that gratitude from a guest was rare. But, earlier that day, the duke had demonstrated a familiarity with his household staff that spoke of a very different attitude. He had shown genuine regard for them, something Annabel doubted her father could even fathom. The baron's interaction with his staff rarely extended beyond barking commands.

"Do you require help bathing, miss?" Mary asked hesitantly. "I can deliver your clothing to be laundered and return directly."

"No, that will not be necessary. I shall see you later, to dress for dinner."

Mary nodded shyly, retreating with a quiet click of the door.

Alone at last, Annabel took in her surroundings. The room was breathtaking. Sky-blue silk covered the walls, trimmed with freshly painted wainscoting. The bed—a massive four-poster—featured mahogany posts carved into palm trees, their gilded feather-like branches forming a canopy crowned with creamy feather finials.

A rich ivory, gold, and sky-blue rug framed a seating area with a striped damask sofa and matching armchairs, all arranged by a low table. Through a far door, Annabel glimpsed an adjoining room just as opulent as this one. Opposite the windows, gilt-framed portraits of Markham ancestors hung in stately grandeur.

Above her, the intricately paneled ceiling, painted in soft whites and creams, gleamed in the late afternoon light. Baydon Hall's Tudor interiors, with their dark timbers and somber cream-painted panels, seemed gloomy compared to Avonmead's airy elegance.

Annabel marveled at how her life had shifted in a single day. She could scarcely believe her daring in coming here.

She approached the copper tub, tested the water with her fingers, and stepped in, letting the warm embrace soothe her aching muscles. Leaning back, she breathed in the lavender-scented steam. Her pulse, racing with excitement since her arrival, refused to settle.

When she closed her eyes, her mind swirled with thoughts of Halmesbury, of his promise, and of the remarkable change in her fortunes.

She startled awake twenty minutes later, the water now cool and her neck aching from an awkward angle. Shaking off the lingering haze of sleep, she washed quickly, dried herself, and tugged on the fresh chemise.

Her limbs felt heavy as she slipped between the cool sheets of the magnificent bed. Exhaustion tugged at her, the culmination of a sleepless night and a month of ceaseless worry. For the first time in weeks, her mind was at ease.

As she drifted into slumber, her thoughts wandered back to her earlier conversation with Halmesbury. Why had he not spoken to Richard in three years?

~

As Philip buttoned his small clothes, he found himself bemused by the unexpected turn his life had taken earlier that day. His thoughts lingered on Annabel Ridley, the remarkable young woman who had so suddenly—and delightfully—changed his course.

Jones handed him his black trousers, but Philip waved them away.

"Jones, I believe something less formal is in order. Miss Ridley does not have proper evening attire for dinner, and I would not wish to embarrass her."

"Of course, Your Grace. Might I suggest day wear to match the lady?"

Philip nodded, and Jones quickly returned with ivory trousers, a navy coat, and a poplin waistcoat.

As Philip stepped into the trousers, he felt a growing anticipation for the evening ahead. He eased his arms into the waistcoat, standing still as the valet tightened it to an exact fit. Raising his chin, he allowed Jones to tie his cravat in an intricate knot; the folds draping elegantly at his throat. Though Philip often avoided such stiff formalities when at Avonmead, tonight felt different. He wanted to look his best for Annabel.

"Will Miss Ridley be staying beyond tonight, Your Grace?" Jones's tone was casual, but his curiosity was evident.

"Miss Ridley will leave in the morning," Philip replied, adjusting his sleeves. "But I hope she will return by the end of the week—this time, as my bride."

Jones's hands stilled briefly before he resumed tying the cravat with practiced efficiency. "Congratulations, Your Grace. Just this morning, you were discussing the marriage mart, yet tonight you have a new duchess in hand."

Philip chuckled softly at the valet's understatement, recognizing the carefully phrased question behind the comment.

"Indeed, Jones. I was most surprised by Miss Ridley's visit. Her timing was impeccable, and I find myself quite taken with her."

Jones paused again, his gaze lifting to meet Philip's. The valet's bespectacled eyes shone warmly. "I am delighted to hear it, Your Grace. It will be uplifting to have a lady in residence once more. Miss Ridley sounds lovely—from what Clinton mentioned earlier." He blanched. "Not that Clinton was gossiping, mind you!"

Philip allowed himself a brief smile. Jones had been with him since his teenage years, and their relationship had grown into one of mutual respect and trust. The valet's well wishes were genuine and deeply appreciated.

"Miss Ridley is indeed lovely," Philip said quietly as Jones retrieved the coat. Sliding his arms into the coat, Philip felt the weight of the fine wool settle over his shoulders. Jones fastened the gilt buttons with deft fingers, then circled him for a final inspection, smoothing the fabric and straightening every detail to his meticulous standards.

"I believe you are ready, Your Grace. Enjoy your dinner."

"Thank you, Jones. I will meet with my man of business before dinner. Please ask Clinton to show him to my study when he arrives."

"Certainly, Your Grace."

"And Jones," Philip added as he prepared to leave, "do not wait up for me tonight. I will undress myself. But I shall see you an hour before sunrise—I will escort Miss Ridley home at first light."

The valet bowed, his satisfaction evident as he stepped back.

Philip exited his rooms, his mind racing with plans. He needed to set arrangements in motion, not only to finalize the matter with Lord Filminster, but also to prepare for his future with Annabel. His steps quickened as his thoughts turned to her—her courage, her wit, her intriguing nature.

The day had brought with it an unexpected joy, a sense of lightness he had not felt in years. As he moved purposefully toward his study to meet with his man of business,

Philip could not help but feel a growing eagerness for what lay ahead.

∼

As the quiet maid, Mary, helped her into an old-fashioned muslin dress, Annabel worked to quell the nervous excitement bubbling within her. The thought of spending an entire evening in the duke's company felt both thrilling and daunting.

What would she talk about?

It was not every day she dined with a duke. Until this morning, she had never even seen a duke, much less spoken with one. She began mentally listing possible topics, but each one struck her as woefully dull.

Perhaps she should recall the conversations she had shared with Richard over the years. He had once told her she was captivating, so surely those topics would suffice. Horses and estate management were safe subjects, and she could always inquire about local customs or upcoming seasonal celebrations.

Her hand settled over her stomach as she fought to quiet the fluttering sensation of nerves. Butterflies seemed to whirl beneath her ribs. If she did not calm herself, she feared she would not be able to eat a bite.

Mary's deft fingers moved quickly, working Annabel's tangle of chestnut hair into a coiffure. Taking a deep breath, Annabel steadied herself.

No matter what happened, she would not ruin this proposal. She would learn everything needed to make the duke proud of her. For reasons she could not fully explain, his opinion mattered now. She wanted him to like her, to be glad he had offered her this chance.

She closed her eyes briefly, her resolve solidifying. She would be a good wife—and a good duchess, though the notion still seemed overwhelming. Such an elevation in status was unexpected when she had only ever hoped for a kind husband and a warm household. Now she faced a future so grand it left her a little breathless.

Mary stepped back and gestured toward the mirror.

Annabel turned, gasping softly at her reflection. The maid had outdone herself, fashioning Annabel's hair into a cascade of chestnut curls that framed her face beautifully. She had never seen her hair styled so elegantly.

The muslin dress, while outdated, was simple and charming, its delicate red flowers embroidered around the hem adding a cheerful touch. The colors suited her, bringing a healthy glow to her cheeks. Annabel tilted her head, taking in the woman staring back at her. She suspected she looked ... attractive.

Still, she worried. The late duchess, with her flawless porcelain complexion, had set an impossibly high standard. Annabel's sun-kissed skin, earned from hours spent riding outdoors, was far from the pale ideal of London fashion. She hoped the duke would not mind.

Her gaze lingered on her reflection. This was who she was—her complexion, her frame, her spirit. She could not change those things, and deep down, she did not wish to.

I am simply Annabel; she thought. *And I must trust that I am enough.*

∞

PHILIP PACED the length of the library, his boots soundless on the Axminster carpeting of rich gold and deep gray. Despite his calm exterior, a current of excitement hummed through him. He ran a hand through his hair in an uncharacteristic display of nerves.

He could not remember the last time he had looked forward to spending time with someone as much as he anticipated this evening with Annabel. She was unlike any woman he had met—warm, genuine, and entirely without artifice. The prospect of her presence thrilled him, even as he reminded himself to temper his behavior. He did not want to overwhelm her or give her any reason to regret her decision to accept his proposal.

The sound of light footsteps echoed from the hall, interrupting his restless thoughts. Drawing a steadying breath, Philip straightened his coat and turned toward the door, schooling his features into a calm smile.

Annabel hesitated on the threshold, framed by the soft light of the sconces lining the hall. She wore an older muslin dress, likely unearthed from his late mother's trunks. Though simple and modest, the gown suited her, its bodice highlighting her natural curves with an effortless grace. Her hair, styled in a cascade of chestnut curls, framed her face beautifully. She looked lovely—so much so that Philip's heart skipped a beat.

Striding forward, he reached for her hand, brushing a light kiss across her gloved fingers as he bowed. A delicate scent of lavender drifted from her, and he forced himself to keep his thoughts—his impulses—in check.

"Your Grace," Annabel said shyly, a small smile playing on her lips, "I must confess to feeling a little mortified this evening."

"Mortified?" Philip asked, arching a brow in mock disbelief.

"I can only imagine what you must think of me—riding alone across two counties to seek you out."

"We have already discussed this, have we not?" Philip replied, his tone light. "You are reckless and daring." He paused, his voice softening. "But despite your teasing to the contrary, promise me that is the last time you do something so dangerous."

Her gaze was earnest as she nodded. "I promise."

"Good. Now promise me you will remain daring, though with a bit more caution."

She gave him a startled look, then broke into a smile. "Daring but not reckless," she agreed.

"Excellent."

"In that vein," she began, her eyes twinkling with humor, "I should know your name if we are to marry."

"Philip. Philip Markham, at your service."

"And do you?" she asked with a playful tilt of her head.

"Do I what?"

"Do you love horses? Your name—it means lover of horses, does it not?"

Her whimsical observation caught him off guard, and he chuckled. She was a puzzle—part country hoyden, part sharp-witted gentlewoman. Every moment spent with her revealed another delightful facet of her personality.

"I do, in fact," he answered, smiling. "Very much."

"I love horses, too," she said warmly. "I ride daily. Avonmead must be a revelation to explore on horseback."

"Then we shall ride together, and I will show you your new estate. Once we marry, you will have access to the finest stables in Wiltshire."

"It is my first visit to this county. In fact, it is the first time I have left Somerset. Today has been quite the adventure."

Philip watched her closely, marveling at her calm demeanor. She had agreed to marry him—a stranger—and yet showed no signs of wavering. She was no timid miss, and her fortitude only strengthened his belief that she was the perfect choice.

"Annabel," he began, "may I call you Annabel?"

"I think it is far too late in the day to stand on ceremony," she teased. "May I call you Philip?"

"I would be delighted." He offered his arm. "Shall we explore the library until dinner is ready?"

As they strolled among the towering shelves, Philip pointed out various sections of books. "Here, we have periodicals—including Ackermann's Repository and The Gentleman's Magazine. It is quite helpful to read back issues when preparing for a Season. That way, one can catch up on the latest trends and topics of interest."

"Does that include the recent issue featuring you?" Annabel asked, her tone teasing.

Philip grimaced. "Yes, it is all a bit embarrassing. Though I suppose I should not complain—it did bring you to Avonmead."

Her cheeks dimpled as she smiled, clearly pleased.

They lingered in conversation, discussing the classical murals adorning the arched ceiling and their shared appreciation of Italian artists. They debated architectural styles—Annabel favoring the features of Avonmead, while Philip championed Gothic elements.

The library, with its eclectic blend of silks and Morocco leather furnishings, delighted Annabel. She marveled at its cozy yet grand design, imagining herself spending countless hours among its treasures.

The rich scent of aged paper and leather surrounded her, soothing and enticing. She realized with a start that this library might be the most enchanting aspect of the wealth and status marriage to Philip could offer.

Before she could voice her admiration, Clinton appeared at the doorway to announce dinner.

As Philip offered his arm once more, Annabel reflected on the day's events. It felt like a dream—a perfect, unexpected dream. And as they left the library, she found herself hoping it would never end.

CHAPTER
FIVE

"With how many things are we upon the brink of becoming acquainted, if cowardice or carelessness did not restrain our inquiries?"

Mary Shelley's Frankenstein

∽

Annabel sat stiffly on the plush velvet squabs of the ducal carriage, her hands fidgeting with the cuffs of her freshly laundered linen shirt. The motion of the carriage, usually soothing, only added to the swirl of thoughts tangling in her mind.

As they neared Filminster, a heavy sense of foreboding settled over her. The past two days had been like a dream—perfect, and far removed from the suffocating reality she had left behind. But now, as the familiar countryside of her home came into view, she feared waking to find it had all been an illusion.

The thought of standing at the altar, Richard waiting

with that smug smile, made her breath catch painfully in her throat. Her stomach twisted into a tight knot.

Breathe, Annabel. In, out. Or is it out, in?

The possibility loomed like a storm cloud: her father could refuse Halmesbury's suit. That thought threatened to spiral into panic.

In, out. Breathe in, breathe out.

Philip's voice interrupted her racing thoughts. "Annabel?"

His hand covered hers, warm and reassuring, halting her nervous tugging at her cuffs.

"Yes, Your Gra—Philip?" She corrected herself, her voice faltering but soft.

~

He smiled softly at her slip. "You must relax, sweet. I will handle everything. Within a few hours, you will be safely home, and I will call on your father to make my suit."

She exhaled shakily, though her lips tilted into a small smile at his calm assurance. "Mrs. Harris will have explained my absence as an illness that kept me in bed. My father will not have checked on me—he rarely does when his routine is undisturbed."

Philip frowned slightly at the bitterness that tinged her voice. "Good. That gives us the advantage. I will delay my arrival to give you time, and the carriage will drop you close to Baydon Hall so you can ride in as though you were never gone. When I arrive at your home, I will distract Lord Filminster with my proposal."

She bit her lip, her nerves obvious. "Do you truly believe he will break his arrangement with Richard?"

"I do." Philip's voice was firm, his gray eyes steady. "My

higher rank and my offer will be irresistible to your father. And as for Richard—he will not dare cross me."

Annabel's shoulders sagged in relief, though her fingers still fidgeted. "I cannot thank you enough. I only wish I could remain here with you."

Philip's chest tightened at her heartfelt words, warmth spreading through him. "I do not want you to worry," he said gently. "This will all be resolved quickly, and soon you will never have to think of Richard again."

Her lips parted, then pressed shut as she blushed. Her gaze dropped to their hands, where his still rested over hers. The sight stirred something deep within him—an urge to reassure her, to see her smile again.

He gave a soft laugh. "I have a question for you, Annabel."

Her eyes lifted, curious. "What is it?"

"Why would the baron not send for a doctor if he believed you were ill?"

Her cheeks turned scarlet, and she averted her eyes. "Um ... the nature of the illness ... Mrs. Harris thought it best to prevent inquiries by saying it was ..."

Realization dawned, and Philip quickly cut her off to save her further embarrassment. "Ah. That was quite resourceful of Mrs. Harris."

Annabel's lips twitched, though her cheeks remained red. "It was necessary."

He hesitated, his gaze thoughtful. He had another question, one that had been pressing on his mind. Despite his desire to proceed cautiously, his instincts urged him forward. If they were to marry, this was a matter he needed to settle in his own mind.

"Annabel," he began, his tone quiet but steady. "May I ask something else?"

"Of course."

Philip shifted slightly, leaning forward. "We have agreed to marry, and I want to be certain that we ... suit." He paused, then continued, his voice lower. "May I seal our agreement with a kiss?"

Her eyes widened, her breath catching for a moment. Philip held himself still, his pulse quickening as he awaited her answer.

Then, with a small nod, she consented.

Relief coursed through him, mingling with a quiet thrill. He moved to sit beside her, careful to give her space. Gently, he raised a hand to her cheek, his thumb brushing against her skin.

"Tell me if you feel uncomfortable," he murmured.

She nodded again, her gaze unwavering as she met his.

Slowly, he leaned in, his lips brushing hers with the barest pressure. Her softness startled him, her warmth drawing him in. He deepened the kiss slightly, lingering just enough to sense her response. When her hands lightly rested on his arms, her tentative touch encouraged him, and he withdrew with care.

∼

Annabel's heart raced as Philip's lips brushed hers, tender yet firm, sparking sensations she had never imagined. Her first kiss was everything she had not known she wanted—soft yet thrilling, his warmth steadying even as her emotions swirled. She felt the quiet confidence of his presence, a contrast to the chaos of her thoughts.

When he deepened the kiss, and she responded instinctively, her hands rising to his arms as she leaned into the moment. His care and respect were in every gentle movement, making her feel cherished and safe.

He drew back slowly, his breath mingling with hers, their foreheads nearly touching. His gray eyes, filled with unspoken emotion, met hers. "I cannot wait to make you my wife, Annabel," he murmured, his voice rough with sincerity.

Her chest tightened, and a soft smile played at her lips. "I am looking forward to it as well," she whispered, her voice steady despite the wild thrum of her heart.

Philip's gaze lingered for a moment before he reluctantly moved back to his seat, leaving a warm void where his nearness had been. Annabel felt the absence keenly, her fingers itching to reach for him again, but she clasped her hands tightly in her lap instead.

The carriage bumped gently along the road, the rhythmic motion grounding her as she tried to compose her thoughts. She glanced at Philip, who seemed deep in thought, his expression calm yet contemplative.

Her cheeks warmed as she replayed the kiss in her mind. *Did I do it right? Did I meet his expectations?* She had never thought herself bold, yet in his presence, she felt a courage she had not known before.

Breaking the silence, Philip turned to her with a soft chuckle. "You seem far away in thought."

"I was just ... marveling at how much has changed in so little time," she admitted, her voice quiet. "It is almost overwhelming."

His smile was reassuring. "Life often takes unexpected turns. But I believe some of those turns lead us exactly where we need to be."

Annabel's heart swelled at his words, and she nodded, finding comfort in his confidence.

The carriage slowed, signaling their approach to the woods near Baydon Hall. Philip shifted, retrieving her hat and coat, which he handed to her with a look of regret that their time together was ending for now.

Once the footman had prepared Starling, Philip helped Annabel into the saddle. His hands lingered briefly at her waist, steadying her, before he stepped back.

"Ride safely, Annabel," he said, his voice low and warm. "I will see you very soon."

She smiled down at him, her cheeks still flushed from their earlier embrace. "Until then, Philip."

With a gentle nudge, Starling moved into a brisk canter, carrying her toward the woods. As the wind cooled her flushed face, Annabel allowed herself a small smile. Despite her nerves and doubts, she felt a growing certainty: her life was changing, and she dared to hope it was for the better.

CHAPTER SIX

"Nothing contributes so much to tranquillize the mind as a steady purpose—a point on which the soul may fix its intellectual eye."

Mary Shelley's Frankenstein

∿

P hilip's heart was still light with the thrill of Annabel's agreement as the carriage rolled to a halt in front of Baydon Hall. The house, a charming Tudor structure, stood with its ivy-clad east wing and diamond-paned windows sparkling in the afternoon sun. Its cheerful appearance seemed to echo the spirit of its captivating young resident.

The parkland surrounding the Hall stretched under an endless blue sky, dotted with stately oaks and promising the quiet beauty of morning rides. He could easily picture Annabel atop her horse, her form poised and confident, her cheeks flushed with the exertion of a brisk canter. The thought brought a smile to his lips.

Their conversation and easy camaraderie during the journey had done much to assure him that Annabel was well-suited to the life awaiting her. She was intelligent, warm, and unexpectedly bold. He was relieved to find her not only willing to meet the challenges ahead but also eager to embrace them. What a remarkable twist of fate to find such a partner in a matter of days, just as he had resigned himself to the tedium of a London Season.

Philip breathed in deeply as the carriage door opened, the scent of fresh grass and the distant call of birds adding to the tranquil charm of the estate. With a nod to the footman, he alighted, a renewed sense of purpose driving his every step. Today, he would lay the foundation for his future, a future that now seemed full of promise and possibility.

∽

Lord Filminster was a small, wiry man with a nervous energy that suggested he spent more time imagining his grandeur than securing it. His slight paunch strained against his ill-fitted waistcoat, and the thinning wisps of graying black hair, combed forward in an attempt at a style, did little to disguise his advancing age. He scurried across the room to meet Philip as if eager to ingratiate himself, bowing deeply on the Anatolian rug beneath his feet.

"Your Grace, what an honor to receive you! This is most unexpected. You must have traveled quite a distance to call on me this afternoon?"

Philip inclined his head. "Indeed, Lord Filminster, I

have been eager to meet with you. I wished to introduce myself without delay."

"Eager, you say?" Filminster's narrow face lit with poorly concealed delight. "It is a rare pleasure to host a man of your standing. Why, only last week, I read about you in *The Gentleman's Magazine*. A fortuitous meeting indeed!"

Philip allowed the man's obsequious nature to wash over him as he followed him to a seating area beneath the wide mullioned windows. Annabel had warned him of her father's fixation on status, a trait Philip found both useful and deeply aggravating. The baron, it seemed, was more concerned with the trappings of rank than the substance required to maintain it. Annabel's life under such a man must have been one of suffocating neglect, the full extent of which Philip could only imagine.

Taking the proffered seat, Philip concealed his irritation as the baron fussed with his own position. He shifted and resettled, crossing and uncrossing his legs, as though rehearsing for an imagined portrait of importance.

Finally, Filminster cleared his throat and fixed Philip with a hopeful gaze. "Your visit is most unexpected, Your Grace. Do I gather that you have a specific purpose in calling upon me?"

"I do. I was recently at the Ashbury ball near Saunton, where I had the great pleasure of meeting your daughter, the Honorable Miss Ridley."

"Annabel?" The baron blinked, clearly startled by this turn in the conversation. "Delightful, you say?"

"Indeed. I found her utterly captivating." Philip's tone was firm, leaving no room for doubt. "In fact, I have come to offer for her hand in marriage. I am prepared to be generous in all respects."

Filminster's mouth opened and closed in rapid succession, his astonishment evident. "Generous, you say?" He struggled to regain composure, his fingers twitching against the armrest.

Philip continued, his voice measured. "This would be my second marriage. I have no children or sisters to provide for, which means you would retain her dowry in its entirety. Moreover, I would secure her—and any children we might have—a considerable settlement from my own funds."

Filminster's eyes gleamed with naked avarice before he masked it with a poorly executed expression of concern. "Your Grace, this is an exceedingly generous offer, but ... Annabel is already betrothed."

"To my cousin, Lord Saunton, who will not oppose me. I am a duke, Lord Filminster, and my position outranks his in every regard. Aligning yourself with my house would only elevate your standing and that of your son, particularly when the time comes for him to find a suitable match."

The baron hesitated, his brow furrowed. "Your Grace, you must understand—it is most irregular to break off an engagement, especially so close to the wedding day."

"Have the banns been posted?" Philip inquired smoothly.

"No! This is a household of standing and we will not be posting banns," Filminster retorted, flustered. "Saunton intends to secure a common license as soon as he returns from London."

"Then no harm is done," Philip replied. "No one need know the full circumstances. Let us move swiftly to secure the appropriate agreements, and all parties will benefit."

"But Saunton—"

"I will handle my cousin," Philip interrupted, his tone sharpened with finality. "You have my word that neither you nor your family will suffer any fallout. Quite the contrary—you will gain a direct connection to one of the most respected titles in the realm."

The baron hesitated, his greed and cowardice warring visibly. "And ... when would you propose this wedding take place?"

"This Saturday. I shall return with a special license in hand."

Filminster gawked. "So soon?"

"Time is of the essence," Philip said firmly. "My solicitor will arrive this very afternoon to finalize the settlements. You will have ample reason to celebrate your good fortune."

The baron's expression shifted as he reached a decision, the lure of status tipping the scales. "Very well, Your Grace. I shall summon my solicitor at once."

Philip could not help the wolfish grin he felt spreading his lips. He smelled victory, and it was triumphantly sweet. How quickly one's life could change. His past had taught him it would change for the worse, with little or no warning. Fate had now intervened to show that it could change for the better in an instant if one were open to seizing the opportunity.

∼

ANNABEL STOOD outside the study door with her ear pressed against it. She should feel guilt over her blatant eavesdropping, but it was the only method of discovering what her father was up to. The baron was not a sparkling conversationalist, despite any inflated ideas of self he might indulge in.

Philip had warned her on the carriage ride that he would have to negotiate to win her, and had apologized for any tactics he might need to employ. He had been concerned that she should not feel disrespected by what he may say. Annabel was warmed by the thought that the Duke of Halmesbury was willing to go to such lengths on her behalf. She had not been the subject of so much single-minded interest since her mother had passed on. An actual duke battling for her hand—she was not sure what to think of it other than ... she liked it. She had no qualms about any strategic maneuvering the duke might use to gain the upper hand.

Annabel heard heavy footfalls echoing on the wooden floors behind her and turned to find Mrs. Harris heading her way. The housekeeper's round face lit in delight at finding her home. Annabel quickly pressed a finger to her lips to shush her. She gestured to the woman to step closer.

"I will find you shortly and update you on all that has happened," she leaned in to whisper.

The housekeeper gave a quick nod and turned away. She motioned toward the kitchens, then made her way back the way she had come, doing her best to dampen the sounds of her footsteps. She looked like an untalented performer playing a thief in a bad pantomime, taking exaggerated steps and holding her arms awkwardly. Annabel shook her head in fond amusement at the older woman's antics before pressing her ear back against the study door.

∽

"And what of the upcoming wedding, Halmesbury?" Lord Filminster asked, leaning forward with an almost eager curiosity. Philip resisted the urge to grimace. It was clear the baron was warming quickly to the idea of becoming father-in-law to a duke.

"When is Saunton due back in Filminster?" Philip asked, his tone calm and businesslike.

"I believe we will see him in a week or so. He is planning on returning from London to obtain the common license and finish the wedding preparations at the end of the month," Filminster replied with a nonchalant wave of his hand.

"Perfect." Philip leaned forward slightly, his voice dropping as though sharing a confidential suggestion. "What Saunton does not know will not hurt him. What say I visit my good friend, the Most Reverend and Right Honorable Charles Manners-Sutton, to arrange for a special license and return within four days? My solicitor will arrive later today to work out the marriage settlements, and I shall return—say ... Saturday morning for the wedding?"

Filminster's eyebrows lifted, clearly impressed by the duke's personal connection to the Archbishop of Canterbury. Exactly as Philip had expected. The baron pursed his lips in thought before voicing his primary concern. "But who will inform Saunton?"

Philip kept his tone reassuring. "My solicitor will arrive shortly. Once we finalize the contracts, I will leave for Canterbury. After the wedding, I will send Higgins to deliver a message informing Saunton that Annabel is married, and any questions may be directed to me. You will not need to address the matter yourself, as the entire arrangement will be complete before he is even aware of it. When next you see him, he will have no choice but to treat you with the respect due to your new circumstances."

The baron visibly relaxed, his shoulders loosening as he absorbed this tidy resolution. Annabel had warned Philip of her father's preference for minimal effort. His primary concerns revolved around his own comfort and advantage.

As long as everything appeared neatly resolved, with no lingering responsibilities, he would yield.

Filminster finally nodded. "As long as Saunton is not a liability, we have an agreement. I will send for my solicitor at once so we can finalize the legalities this afternoon."

Philip quelled the triumph rising within him, ensuring his features betrayed nothing but polite satisfaction. Annabel was his.

∽

As Philip exited the study alongside the butler, a curious sensation of being watched struck him. Turning his head, he spotted Annabel peeking around a nearby doorway. Amusement flickered through him as he gestured for the elderly butler to proceed without him. "I will join you shortly," he said, his voice composed. Once the servant disappeared down the hall, Philip motioned Annabel forward.

She moved quickly to meet him, her muslin day dress swaying as she came to a halt before him. Her hand lightly rested on his forearm—a gesture that was both tentative and surprisingly possessive. She looked up at him, her golden-brown eyes wide with worry, her voice lowered so as not to be overheard. "I could not hear the last few moments of your discussion. Has he agreed?"

Philip allowed himself a faint smile, meant to reassure her. "He has agreed. I am heading upstairs with your man, Stedman, to freshen up before we complete the marriage settlements. I had to promise to take responsibility should Saunton protest."

Her eyes widened slightly. "Is that truly a concern?"

"It is highly unlikely. The last thing Saunton would

want is the public scandal that would follow. No, by Saturday morning, you will be my wife, and Saunton will simply have to accept that he has lost."

Annabel exhaled slowly, her shoulders softening as visible relief washed over her. "I can scarcely believe it. You have made everything right. I am free of him." She glanced down at her hands for a moment before meeting his gaze again. "You are my hero," she said, her voice hushed but fervent.

A warmth Philip had not expected swelled within him at her words. Her earnest gratitude and trust were disarming. She had a charm about her—an unpolished but undeniable radiance that made him want to ensure she never regretted placing her faith in him. Silently, he resolved to tread carefully, giving her the space she needed to grow comfortable in their new relationship.

With a gentle touch, he lifted her chin, meeting her soft gaze as he bent to press a light, lingering kiss to her forehead. "I will return Saturday morning," he said, his voice steady. "Until then, promise me—no more midnight escapades. I want you safe when I return."

Annabel's lips quirked into a mischievous smile. "I will consider it," she teased, her tone light but fond. "As long as you promise to be on time for the ceremony."

Philip chuckled softly. "I would not dare be late."

With a last glance, he turned and strode down the hall, leaving her with a grin that lingered at the corners of her lips. Saturday could not come soon enough.

―※―

Mrs. Harris was preparing tea when Annabel walked into the kitchen. Her plump cheeks wreathed in a wide smile. "I am so happy you are bac—feeling better, miss." The older woman corrected herself just in time, mindful of maintaining the pretense that Annabel had been unwell and confined to her room. Her sharp hazel eyes darted to the cook and two maids bustling in the background before returning to Annabel. "I expect you want your tea, miss. Shall I bring it to the library?" She gave an exaggerated wink, her lack of subtlety bringing a fond smile to Annabel's face.

"That would be perfect, Mrs. Harris. And bring some pastries, if you would."

Annabel was not particularly fond of sweets, but Mrs. Harris adored them, and Annabel had long since made a habit of ordering pastries just to indulge her.

As Annabel made her way to the cozy library on the first floor of Baydon Hall, she marveled that soon she would have access to ten times as many books at Avonmead. Settling into a comfortable velvet sofa near the fireplace, she allowed herself a moment to revel in the thought before Mrs. Harris entered, bearing a tea tray.

"Close the door, Mrs. Harris," Annabel said in a raised voice, making sure anyone nearby would hear. "I wish to discuss something." Once the door clicked shut, she gestured for the housekeeper to sit beside her. Pouring tea with practiced ease, she pressed a plate of pastries into Mrs. Harris's reluctant hands.

"I really should not, my girl," Mrs. Harris protested half-heartedly.

"We can argue for several minutes, or you can accept them now so that I can tell you my news."

With a resigned sigh, the older woman settled onto the sofa and took a sugar biscuit from the plate. Her expression softened as she savored the treat, a testament to the cook's renowned skill.

"I found His Grace. He was not what I expected." Annabel hesitated, her thoughts lingering on the duke's surprising kindness and the warm confidence in his manner.

Mrs. Harris bobbed her head, her eyes encouraging Annabel to continue as she chewed thoughtfully.

"He offered to marry me in Lord Saunton's stead."

Mrs. Harris choked on her crumbs, her eyes wide with disbelief. After a few sputtering moments, she found her voice. "The Duke of Halmesbury asked you to be his wife?"

"That is correct."

"And what did you say?"

Annabel took a deep breath. "It is all arranged. Phili—that is, His Grace has already spoken with the baron, and we will wed on Saturday morning."

Mrs. Harris stared at her, her expression a mixture of astonishment and pride. "What would your dear mama say to her Annabel marrying a duke? Is he a good man?"

"A wonderful man," Annabel replied earnestly. "Intelligent, generous, and,"—her voice softened—"handsome. I believe we will have a pleasant future together." She caught herself, realizing how fanciful she sounded, and quickly added, "He is marrying to fulfill his duty, and I am fortunate to be the one he chose. I must remember that this is a practical arrangement."

Mrs. Harris shook her head in wonderment. "What else did he say?"

Annabel's face brightened. "I think I can convince him to bring you on as his housekeeper."

"Me? For a duke?" Mrs. Harris's hand flew to her chest, her astonishment plain.

"He recently gave up his housekeeper to run a charity. The position is vacant, and he said I may help choose a replacement. I want to recommend you. We could stay together, Mrs. Harris. Mama would have been so pleased."

Mrs. Harris looked aghast, though her hazel eyes shone with affection. "But, my girl, a duke's household must be enormous."

"It will be more work than Baydon Hall, but you are more than capable. Please say you will come."

"My dear girl," Mrs. Harris said fondly, shaking her head, "I would follow you to the ends of the earth."

Annabel chuckled. "Father more than makes up for your indulgence. He says no often enough for two parents."

"My girl is going to be a duchess." Mrs. Harris sighed in amazement.

"His Grace will return Saturday morning for the wedding, so we must begin packing."

Mrs. Harris's brow furrowed. "Has the baron spoken to you yet?"

"Not yet. How long do you think it will take for him to inform me of my impending marriage, considering the duke has been here for over an hour?"

Mrs. Harris laughed. "He will inform you just before dinner, I'll wager. In the meantime, I'll sort out your trunks."

Annabel smiled her thanks but paused as Mrs. Harris added, "Caroline wrote. She is well situated in her new position."

Annabel's smile faded. "Good."

"I still do not understand why you helped her after what she did."

Annabel's voice softened. "I cannot hate her, Mrs. Harris. She made a terrible mistake, but she was with us for ten years. If I had cast her out, she would have had no one. Mama would have approved of my decision."

Mrs. Harris nodded, though her expression remained troubled. "You are too forgiving, my girl."

"Perhaps. But I would rather regret my kindness than my cruelty."

Mrs. Harris reached over to pat her hand. "Your mother would be proud of you, Annabel."

Annabel smiled, her thoughts turning to the duke. She had been granted a second chance, and she would not squander it. The duke had granted her a reprieve. Now some other unfortunate debutante would be left with the faithless Lord Saunton. "Please Lord, help the poor miss who takes Richard Balfour as a husband," Annabel prayed under her breath.

CHAPTER SEVEN

"Beware; for I am fearless, and therefore powerful."

Mary Shelley's Frankenstein

∼

FRIDAY, THE EVE BEFORE THE HALMESBURY AND RIDLEY WEDDING.

The past days had been a whirlwind of activity at Baydon Hall as the unexpected Saturday morning nuptials approached. It was late in the evening when Annabel sighed her relief to sink into the sofa in her bedchamber.

"Child, are you in there?" called Mrs. Harris from the open door.

"Yes, Mrs. Harris, come in."

Annabel looked up as the rotund housekeeper closed the door behind her and made her way over. "I thought we might talk. Your mother, bless her heart, would have wanted to have this talk with you on the eve of your wedding. I know it's not my place, but I also know if your dear mama is looking down on us right now, it would please her that someone was here to talk to you."

"Please sit, Mrs. Harris. Do not stand on ceremony with me. We are friends. You are more my family than my own father."

Mrs. Harris's eyes glowed with love as she lowered herself onto the sofa. "Tomorrow morning you wed, young lady."

Annabel beamed in response.

"My girl, there are things you need to know about your wedding night. I am afraid I must be the one to tell you, as your beloved mama cannot. Since she passed when you were so little, I know she never had this talk with you."

"I think I know some basics as I have read some of the animal husbandry texts in the library," Annabel admitted, her cheeks pinking. "But I cannot say I know exactly what to expect. Lord Saunton and Caroline were ... well ... indiscreet, but I fear there must be more to it than that. I would appreciate your counsel. Though..." She looked away, her voice faltering with embarrassment. "... this is a most awkward discussion."

Mrs. Harris coughed delicately, a faint blush tinging her own cheeks. "Indeed, young lady. I have only had this talk once before with my daughter, many years ago. And I buried my husband before I came to Baydon Hall, so I may be rusty on the subject."

Annabel nodded her encouragement.

"What do you think you know, child?" Mrs. Harris continued.

The housekeeper stayed with Annabel for close to an hour. Annabel asked many questions, and the older woman answered with gentle candor, doing her best to prepare the young bride. When Mrs. Harris finally took her leave, Annabel reflected fondly on their shared history. Mrs. Harris had become a motherly figure to her since her mother's passing, and she would dearly love for the duke to offer her the position of housekeeper at Avonmead. Mrs. Harris was one of the few aspects of her life at Baydon Hall that she would miss. Her presence would bring much-needed comfort and familiarity as Annabel embarked on her new life.

Alone with her thoughts, Annabel drifted into a reverie. Her dreams of making a love match with Richard now seemed a lifetime ago. She could scarcely believe how much had changed in just a month.

She curled her legs beneath her night rail, her slippers discarded on the floor. Unbidden, memories of Richard came to her, a bittersweet echo of her younger self's foolish dreams.

"Why are you crying, Annabel?"

"The other girls said I laugh too much. They said if I had a mother to teach me how to behave, I would know better. They do not wish to play with me anymore. And Father says I am an unfashionable piece who will never attract a decent husband."

"Annabel, they are silly, jealous girls who don't know how to make their own happiness like you do. Forget them, and I will be your friend. As for your father, he is a vainglorious fool who knows nothing of fashion. Why, he wears one of those atrocious eye lockets, and I don't believe it's even an image of your mother's eye?"

Annabel had fallen in love with Richard on the spot. He had always been kind to her, including her in his adventures when he visited her brother.

Her tears dried as she gave him a cheeky smile. "You are correct. The eye locket is of his grandmother."

Richard burst out laughing. "That is perfect! Now, young lady, are you going to go riding with me?"

Annabel shook her head to dispel the memory. She had once thought Richard perfect, but she now saw his flaws clearly. His betrayal had crushed her infatuation. Love, she realized, involved trust and understanding. It decidedly did not involve indiscretions with a maid in the stables.

It was time to focus on making a success of her new circumstances. Philip was different—genuine, steady, kind. She believed him when he had promised fidelity and partnership. Their relationship might not have the passionate intensity she had once dreamed of, but it could grow into something deep and meaningful. She could not deny that the duke stirred her senses and her mind.

The absence of her brother Brendan at her wedding saddened her. Yet, as her father refused to discuss him or his whereabouts, she would have to embrace her new life without him. She silently resolved to find Brendan someday, to reunite with the sibling who had once been her closest confidant.

Her thoughts turned to Philip again. He did not crave admiration or social acclaim like Richard. Instead, he focused on improving his lands, serving his tenants, and championing the needs of his community. In their brief time together, they had shared meaningful discussions, discovering a harmony in their beliefs.

As she gazed into the soft glow of the hearth, Annabel allowed herself a small, daring hope.

Might she and her duke grow to love one another?

It was midmorning when Philip rode up to the front of Baydon Hall, just four days after meeting with Filminster to ask for Annabel's hand. He had a special license burning a hole in his breast pocket and anticipation beating in his chest. His travels over the past few days had culminated in spending the night at the local inn. As he had not taken the time to return to Avonmead, he hoped Annabel would not mind his informal riding attire. He wore a wool coat over his buckskins with his favorite Hessian boots—the same clothing he had worn the day they met. His private carriage would not arrive until this morning, directly at Baydon Hall. Theirs was to be a small ceremony with the local vicar, the baron, and upper servants serving as witnesses, so he trusted his attire would not be viewed as disrespectful.

His carriage should have arrived by now, but as he approached the front entrance, he noticed that the carriage currently stopped in front of the Hall did not bear his coat of arms. Instead, it displayed the Saunton coat of arms gilded on the door—a fact confirmed as his cousin stepped down from the shadowed interior.

Philip brought his chestnut gelding to a stop and dismounted. A stable hand rushed forward as if expecting him, doffing his cap as he took the reins to lead Gentleman's Boon down the drive toward the rear.

Richard Balfour, his cousin and former best friend, turned at the noise. His face registered surprise. "Halmesbury? What are you doing here?"

"I could ask the same. I thought you were in London."

Richard's emerald green eyes swept over Philip's riding apparel as he responded. "I had personal business to take care of. My betrothed"—Richard gestured at the manor's front door—"Miss Ridley, deserves some extra attention as I... I may have upset her a little recently."

Philip lifted a brow at this euphemistic understatement. "Hmm... I don't know how to tell you this, old chap, but Annabel is no longer your betrothed."

Richard frowned before his face cleared, and he recovered his aplomb. His characteristic devil-may-care grin spread across his too-handsome countenance. Richard had always reminded him of Lord Byron with his sable hair, poetic looks, and soulful eyes. He had to concede the appeal; Jane had certainly preferred the earl's appearance over Philip's own hard edges and more earnest charms. "That old codger would never agree to relinquish a connection to an earl. What would you know about it, anyway?"

"The old codger decided a duke was a far more enticing prospect."

Richard's eyes narrowed as he faced his cousin down. "What are you saying, Halmesbury?"

"I am saying that Filminster knows I would make a better son-in-law than you."

The earl's face reflected confusion before settling into an angry mask. "You scheming—What have you done?" Richard exclaimed, turning to stride up the stairs, where he pounded on the heavy door.

When the elderly butler opened it, his faded blue eyes rounded, flabbergasted at finding both the earl and the duke framed in the aperture. He swiftly adopted a stiff expression as Lord Saunton demanded to see Annabel.

"Allow me to show you to the drawing room, my lord. Your Grace." He bowed politely to each of them and turned to lead them down the corridor in a brisker manner than Philip had noticed on his prior visit. It would appear the servant was eager to show them in so he might speed up his departure from their menacing presence.

Philip fumed as he walked alongside Saunton, following the butler past the wood-paneled walls carved with arcane symbolism and the tall balustrades of the climbing staircase. Neither man paid any attention to the ornate designs as they marched down the hall, bristling with hostility. Philip was gripped by a surge of territorial energy, suppressing his instinct to fight. Saunton's presence was causing his blood to boil. This was his day with Annabel, and he would not allow his cousin's unexpected presence to ruin the wedding or Annabel's humor. He needed to address this debacle swiftly before it interrupted his plans. He was taking his bride home with him this day, no matter what Richard Balfour had to say about it.

When they reached the drawing room, the butler held the door open for them. As soon as they entered, the servant made a hasty departure. The door thumped closed in his enthusiasm to leave them behind.

Philip prowled over to the large, intricate stone fireplace. Leaning an elbow on the mantelpiece, he turned to contain his fuming by glaring out the mullioned windows to the westerly gardens beyond. It would not do to engage with Richard at this moment because their unanticipated encounter could turn into a brawl with very little provocation. He had not been in the mountebank's presence since the night his late wife had passed on and he did not trust himself to speak yet. Not delaying the wedding needed to remain foremost in his mind, irrespective of his grievances from the past.

∽

Annabel paced back and forth in the library, her heart lifting as Stedman knocked and entered—then sinking as she took in the butler's uncharacteristically flustered demeanor. Stedman, always so composed, hesitated, his Adam's apple bobbing as he swallowed before speaking.

"The Duke of Halmesbury is in the drawing room." He paused, looking momentarily unsure of himself. "... with Lord Saunton."

Annabel froze, the air suddenly heavy with tension. Behind her, the baron let out a startled grunt, his face twisting in alarm. "This will not do. This will not do at all. Halmesbury promised I would not have to speak with the earl!"

Annabel pressed her lips together, holding back the sharp retort that danced on the edge of her tongue. This was hardly the moment to remind her father of his tendency to hide from difficult situations. She turned to face him, taking in his agitated state—his rounded belly jiggling as he shifted from one scrawny leg to the other, his thin shoulders hunched in nervous energy.

"Why don't I go speak with the gentlemen to sort this out, Father?" she offered, keeping her tone calm and conciliatory.

The baron stopped his bouncing, planting his hands on his hips as he considered her suggestion.

Out of the corner of her eye, Annabel caught a glimpse of the vicar, who had taken refuge on the overstuffed sofa. He seemed to have suddenly developed a keen interest in the gardens beyond the diamond-paned windows, his gaze fixed firmly outside. She did not recall him being so devoted to horticulture in their previous meetings.

After a long pause, the baron nodded with an air of affected grandeur. "Yes, that seems wise. They will both wish to speak to you, and I see no need to involve myself prematurely. I shall remain here and entertain the vicar while you address the situation."

The words were delivered as if he were doing her a great favor. Annabel suppressed a sigh, schooling her features into a composed smile. "Of course, Father. I shall take care of it."

She turned toward the door, smoothing her skirts as she gathered her thoughts. The baron's lack of fortitude was nothing new, and she could hardly fault him for relying on her. Halmesbury had gone to great lengths on her behalf, and it seemed only fair that she do her part now.

Squaring her shoulders, Annabel resolved to face whatever awaited her in the drawing room with grace and determination.

CHAPTER EIGHT

"Nothing is so painful to the human mind as a great and sudden change."

Mary Shelley's Frankenstein

~

Annabel shored up her courage as she stood outside the drawing-room door. Since Stedman had informed her that both her former betrothed and her new one were waiting together, her nerves had been in turmoil. She drew a deep, fortifying breath, steeling herself for the encounter she had hoped to avoid.

Philip believes you are bold, she reminded herself. That thought, both a challenge and an encouragement, gave her the final push to open the door. *You must take what you want, Annabel. No one will hand it to you.*

As she entered, her gaze immediately sought Philip's tall, comforting presence. Over the last few days, she had come to appreciate his steady composure and thoughtful encouragement. Richard, with his charm and affability, had once captivated her, but it was Philip's strength and sincerity that now felt like a safe harbor. And her traitorous inner voice added, *It does not hurt that he is as handsome as a Greek god.*

The two men stood at opposite ends of the stone fireplace. Richard, with his dark, rakish charm, appeared every inch the social favorite he had always been, but beside Philip, he seemed less substantial. Philip, taller and broader, exuded quiet power. His golden hair and calm gray eyes gave him an aura of dependability that made her feel anchored just looking at him.

Richard stepped forward, his expression dark. "How do you even know my cousin?" he demanded sharply. "You barely leave the Hall, with that weak fool of a father of yours too afraid to even board a carriage."

Annabel glanced at Philip. He gave her the barest of nods, his silent encouragement bolstering her confidence. "I knew of His Grace's reputation," she answered evenly. "He is known for helping people in need, so I sought his assistance."

Richard's jaw dropped. "You approached him? *Called on him?*"

Annabel nodded, meeting his gaze.

"But Avonmead is nearly a full day's ride on horseback!"

She inclined her head again.

Richard's face paled as the realization dawned. "You rode there—alone?"

"Yes."

"You rode across two counties in those infernal breeches of yours?"

"Precisely," she said, her voice steady. "I told you I would do whatever it took to end our betrothal."

Richard's complexion darkened with anger, his voice rising. "You reckless fool! You could have been killed—or worse."

Annabel's brow furrowed. "Yes, that is what His Grace also said. Although I fail to understand what could be worse."

Richard threw his hands in the air, pacing a few steps before turning back to her. His voice shook with frustration. "Worse is why you should never have gone! A girl caught alone in the countryside could pray for the sweet release of death rather than endure what might befall her."

Annabel instinctively stepped back, giving him a wary look. "Then perhaps you should not have driven me to such extremes," she retorted, her voice soft but firm. "I had to turn to a stranger because you, the man who claimed to care for me, showed no regard for my thoughts or feelings."

Richard's temper flared again. "You would have been a countess! A wealthy woman with five estates to command. What more could you want?"

Annabel's composure wavered, her voice trembling with raw emotion. "All I wanted was your regard, Richard. Your respect. Your love."

"I *do* care for you!" he exclaimed. "I have never been willing to marry anyone else. I went to great lengths to make this match happen."

Her lips curled in incredulity. "What lengths, pray?"

"I escorted you to those tedious country dances. I called on your father—repeatedly—and endured his dull conversation at countless dinners. I even arranged for a celebrated modiste to come all the way from London to outfit you for your new role!"

Annabel's temper flared, her control snapping under the weight of his self-centered words. "You are insufferable!" she cried, her voice sharp with indignation. "Everything you've done has been for your own vanity. You live for your own pleasures, Richard, and you do not care about my happiness in the least. I would rather remain unmarried forever than become your wife."

∾

PHILIP WATCHED his betrothed and her former betrothed flinging words back and forth. A tense atmosphere thickened the air, the passionate exchange prickling something that could have been jealousy in his chest. A surge of impatience pushed him forward; Annabel was his bride, and there would be no further entanglement with Richard Balfour. Not today. Not ever.

"Enough!" His voice cut through the tension like a blade. Startled, both Annabel and Richard turned to him, where he leaned against the elaborately carved stone fireplace, his stance commanding the room.

"Richard, why are you so adamant about marrying Annabel?" Philip asked. He was about to seize an opportunity for honesty that bordered on cruelty, but he told himself it was necessary. The sooner Annabel realized love was an illusion, the easier it would be to build a foundation of partnership and understanding with her—one based on practicality, not romantic idealism.

Richard crossed his arms and gave his cousin a long, calculating look. "I like Annabel. And if I am to be legshackled to a woman for the rest of my life, it would be nice if we got along."

Philip's heart clenched at Annabel's audible gasp. Her soft features contorted with disbelief and hurt, and it took every ounce of his willpower not to cross the room and tug her into his arms. She deserved better. He would give her better. "That is an inadequate answer," Philip said coolly. "Annabel has chosen me—" He thumped his chest with a clenched fist, the gesture forceful. "—in your stead."

Richard's expression darkened, his green eyes flaring with anger. "You're doing this to seek vengeance against me for Jane. How many times must I tell you? Nothing happened between us!"

Philip's gray gaze narrowed. "This is about Annabel, not Jane. That my involvement irks you is merely a delightful bonus."

Annabel's brows furrowed, and she looked back and forth between the men, confusion flickering across her face. Philip cursed himself for letting their sordid history surface. Quickly, he veered the conversation back on track.

"Miss Ridley deserves better than coercion and betrayal," Philip said firmly. "As an act of honor, I offered her my name and protection. Annabel will be mistress of Avonmead. You would do well to respect that."

Richard let out a short, derisive laugh. "What right do you have to interfere?"

"The right Annabel granted me when you proved yourself unworthy. Shall I recount the details of your disgrace in the stables, or will you concede this outcome is your doing?"

Annabel stiffened at the mention of the stables, her gaze dropping momentarily to her gloved hands. Richard stepped closer to her, his voice low but desperate. "Is this what you want, Annabel? To marry Philip?"

She hesitated, but when her brandy eyes lifted to meet Philip's steady gaze, her resolve solidified. "Yes," she said softly but firmly. "This is what I want."

Richard's face twisted with frustration. "Annabel,

you're making a mistake. My dear cousin has secrets. He's not telling you the full truth about why he is marrying you."

Philip stepped forward, his presence imposing. "Enough, Richard," he warned, his tone as sharp as the crack of a whip. "This matter is settled. If you value what little dignity you have left, I suggest you leave before you make an even greater fool of yourself."

Richard ran a hand through his dark curls, visibly shaken. For a long moment, he looked at Annabel with a mix of longing and regret. Then, finally, he exhaled a shaky breath. "I wish you all the best, Annabel. I did plan to treat you well, and I hope you find happiness."

He took her hand, his lips brushing her fingers in a lingering kiss. Philip's jaw tightened, a low growl of displeasure rumbling in his throat. Richard straightened, snorting disgust as he turned to his cousin. "Enjoy your victory, Halmesbury. But mark my words—you will regret this."

"You had your chance, Saunton," Philip said coldly. "And you ruined it."

With that, Richard turned and stormed out, the heavy door slamming shut behind him.

Philip exhaled slowly, his shoulders relaxing as the tension dissipated. When he looked back at Annabel, he noted the dazed expression on her face. He crossed the room, taking her hands in his. "Do not let this unpleasantness ruin our day," he said gently. "What say you to getting married and beginning our new life at Avonmead?"

Her lips curved into a small, tentative smile. The first since the confrontation began. "I think I would like that very much," she replied.

Philip bent to press a soft kiss to her forehead, a wave of protectiveness surging within him. "I have been looking forward to this moment since we parted," he said, his voice low and earnest. "I cannot wait to call you my wife."

As they left the drawing room together, Philip vowed to himself that he would give Annabel a life of security and care. Whatever ghosts lingered from his past would not touch her. She deserved happiness, and he intended to see that she found it. They made their way to the library where her father, Stedman, and Mrs. Harris were waiting for them with the vicar, but Philip remained worried, hoping Annabel would not pay heed to the hints regarding Jane's betrayal.

The betrayal you drove her to, whispered his treacherous conscience.

~

THE CEREMONY PASSED by Annabel in a haze. Her mind raced with the strange comments Richard had made about Jane Markham. Why had Richard and Philip not spoken in three years? Had the late duchess's passing, which she recalled was about three years ago, played a role? Were the two events connected? A sense of unease gnawed at her. Was there some hidden reason behind the duke's resolve to marry her?

The vicar's steady voice broke through her thoughts.

"Wilt thou have this woman to thy wedded wife, to live together after God's ordinance in the holy estate of Matrimony? Wilt thou love her, comfort her, honor, and keep her, in sickness and in health; and, forsaking all other, keep thee only unto her, so long as ye both shall live?"

Annabel's eyes lifted to meet Philip's gaze. His gray eyes, full of sincerity, held hers with unwavering intensity.

"I will," he said in his deep baritone, the sound sending

a shiver down her spine and settling a warmth deep in her chest.

She drew in a steadying breath and offered him a small smile, reassured by his presence. She trusted him more than she had ever trusted Richard. Unlike his charming yet duplicitous cousin, this man had a reputation for generosity and honor. He had acted decisively to help her. She could not let Richard's bitter accusations cloud her judgment.

Yet, the quarrel had planted seeds of doubt. What if Philip had secrets of his own? She reminded herself that theirs was a marriage of convenience, not romance. She had no right to expect more than what they had agreed upon. Whatever deeper feelings stirred within her, she must guard them carefully. The duke had already known and lost great love—his late duchess had been that for him.

A murmur rippled through the room. Startled, Annabel realized the vicar had paused. All eyes were on her. Mrs. Harris raised a questioning brow. Stedman regarded her with stern expectancy. Even the vicar gave a faint cough to prompt her, and Philip's concerned expression made her heart squeeze.

She had missed her cue.

Frustrated with herself for allowing her thoughts to wander, Annabel quickly recovered and spoke. "I will."

The relief on Philip's face was fleeting but evident, his warm smile returning as he gazed down at her. His presence steadied her once more.

As the vows resumed, Philip slipped the ring onto her finger, his touch firm yet gentle. When he gave her hand a reassuring squeeze, a wave of calm settled over her.

Curse Richard and his venomous words. She would not let his bitterness ruin this moment. He was simply spiteful over losing their battle of wills. His accusations were merely an attempt to plant mistrust where none should exist.

This was her wedding day, and she stood by her choice.

There were no dark secrets to be revealed.

∿

Philip ate his cake in a mild state of euphoria, the flavor barely registering as he savored the realization that he was now married to the daring Miss Ridley—now the Duchess of Halmesbury. Days of hasty planning had culminated in this momentous occasion, securing Annabel as his wife. The future stretched ahead, promising companionship and shared purpose. He allowed himself a moment to marvel at her seated beside him, her feminine presence a balm to the turbulence of the past few days.

Richard's arrival had been an unwelcome surprise, but the matter was settled. Annabel, mercifully, remained unaware of the painful past shared by himself, Richard, and the late duchess. This day belonged to them alone, and he was determined to ensure her happiness moving forward.

He felt Annabel's hand rest lightly on his, her touch warm and grounding. He turned to meet her gaze, and those enchanting brandy-colored eyes met his own. A blend of gold and brown, her eyes held an inner light that seemed to glow even brighter now. She was radiant in her muslin day dress adorned with delicate embroidered flowers. She had captivated him from the start, and he found himself grateful once more for her courage in seeking him out.

"Philip," she whispered, leaning closer as the baron and the vicar carried on their conversation. "I know this may not be the best moment, but I wish to speak with you about Mrs. Harris before we leave."

"Mrs. Harris?" He blinked, pulling himself back to the present. His thoughts had wandered toward the journey ahead, the new life they would begin together, and the countless moments he hoped to share with her.

"The baron's housekeeper," Annabel clarified.

Her words made him pause. He had noticed how she rarely referred to Filminster as her father, calling him instead "the baron." It was a telling detail of her life here—one marked by loneliness and emotional distance. The notion made him even more determined to ensure she found warmth and belonging as the mistress of Avonmead.

Annabel's voice brought him back from his musings. "We are quite close. I know this is very forward, but I would like to offer her a position at Avonmead, if you agree. She has been a great comfort to me. I thought this might be a good time to address it, so she can make arrangements."

Philip's face softened at the suggestion. He recalled Mrs. Harris from the ceremony earlier, the cheerful, round woman dabbing at her eyes with a handkerchief. That someone in this lonely household had cared for Annabel deeply touched him. He had no objection to welcoming the woman to Avonmead if it meant bringing a piece of Annabel's comfort along with her.

A grin spread across his face as he saw the nervousness in hers. On this day, she could have asked him for anything, and he would have gladly given it. If bringing Mrs. Harris brought his new wife joy, then so be it.

Leaning closer to ensure their conversation remained private, he whispered, "For you, my lovely wife, anything. Anything at all."

He sealed the promise with a soft kiss to her forehead, content to see her smile widen in return.

CHAPTER NINE

"Invention, it must be humbly admitted, does not consist in creating out of void, but out of chaos."

Mary Shelley's Frankenstein

~

Mrs. Harris and Annabel stood wrapped in a heartfelt embrace. They had stolen a moment in the study to say their goodbyes, and both were struggling to speak without tears spilling over.

"You will make arrangements to join me at Avonmead?" Annabel asked softly.

"Yes, Your Grace. I will join you as soon as possible. I wish I were leaving with you now. It will be lonely here without you."

Annabel snorted in disagreement. "What happened to 'my girl'? Or 'child'? What is this 'Your Grace' nonsense?"

The housekeeper's warm hazel eyes glistened with unshed tears as she chuckled and released Annabel. "You are no longer a child. It is time to recognize you as a grown woman. A duchess of consequence now. You will have to hire tutors or a governess and whatnot to learn all the new airs you will need in polite society. I will have to learn to curtsy to you."

"No airs with you, Mrs. Harris. And no curtsies ... unless we are in company. Is that how it works? Do upper servants curtsy to duchesses? Oh my, I have so much to learn before I attempt to venture out into polite society!"

The older woman's broad face lit with a smile, her rosy cheeks plumping up with affection. "I cannot tell you much about polite society. I am a country housekeeper for a reclusive baron who never goes anywhere. Best I can tell you is to take care of yourself until I get to Avonmead. You hear me, my girl? And take care of that handsome husband of yours."

Annabel thrilled at the mention of Philip. She was married now, beginning a new life filled with possibilities. The future stretched ahead, bright and promising, and she felt capable of facing it all with Halmesbury at her side.

"Mrs. Harris, I cannot wait for you to join me! Let me hide you in one of my trunks. No one will know you are in there. Say yes, and we will sneak you into the second carriage!"

Mrs. Harris chuckled. "These old bones won't fit into a trunk. We will have to wait. Perhaps His Grace will make the arrangements before Christmas, and we will be together for the holidays."

Annabel sighed with playful frustration. "There you go, being practical. No sense of adventure..." she teased. She took a step back and bent her knees into a deep curtsy to the widow who had become a mother to her. "Until we meet again, Mrs. Harris."

"Until we meet again, Your Grace, the Duchess of Halmesbury." With a curtsy in reply and a cheeky grin, the housekeeper turned and left the room.

∼

As the carriage rolled forward, Annabel drew a shaky breath. It was done. She was married, and now she was alone with Philip, her husband. The realization sent a wave of nervous anticipation through her, leaving her both exhilarated and uncertain. She had made the leap into a new life, trusting this man who had offered her safety and companionship in place of the betrayal she had left behind.

Philip seemed to sense her apprehension. He leaned forward slightly, his gray eyes warm as they met hers. "You are quiet, my sweet," he said softly, his voice carrying a soothing cadence.

"I was just thinking," she murmured, lowering her gaze briefly before daring to look back at him. "Everything has happened so quickly."

"It has," he agreed, reaching out to take her hand. His touch was firm but gentle, his thumb brushing over her gloved knuckles. "But I do not regret a moment of it. Do you?"

Annabel hesitated, her heart thudding. "No," she said at last. "I do not regret it."

His smile deepened, and he lifted her hand to his lips, pressing a lingering kiss to her fingers. The tenderness of the gesture sent a warmth blooming in her chest. "Then let us not dwell on what is behind us," he said. "Today is a beginning."

Her lips curved into a tentative smile, and she nodded. "A beginning," she echoed.

Philip's expression softened further as he regarded her. "Annabel," he began, his tone taking on a new gravity. "There is much I hope to share with you in the days and weeks to come. I hope we can build something strong together—something real."

She was struck by the sincerity in his words, her nerves easing slightly as his hand remained steadfast around hers. "I hope for that too," she whispered.

He shifted closer, his free hand rising to tuck a loose strand of her hair behind her ear. His touch was fleeting, yet it sent her heart racing. "Good," he said, his voice low but steady. "Because I intend to do everything in my power to make you happy, Annabel."

She believed him. In his gaze, she saw determination and care, and it steadied her in ways she had not expected. This was no reckless union of passion or mere convenience. There was potential here—a future built on trust and mutual respect.

Philip's hand lingered against her cheek for a moment before he withdrew slightly, giving her space. "We have a long journey ahead," he said lightly, breaking the charged silence. "But I find myself eager for the destination."

Annabel's smile grew. "As am I," she admitted.

Settling back into their seats, the couple allowed the gentle sway of the carriage to carry them forward, leaving behind doubts and fears as they began their journey together. Annabel's heart was lighter, her trust in Philip solidifying with every passing moment.

As the countryside blurred past the windows, she could not help but wonder what the future held. Whatever it might be, she was ready to face it—with Philip at her side.

Philip leaned back against the squabs of the carriage, his gaze fixed on his new bride seated across from him. Annabel was staring out the window, her hands fidgeting with the fabric of her gown. Her nervous energy was palpable, and it tugged at him in an unexpectedly tender way.

She was his wife now. The thought filled him with a satisfaction he had not anticipated. For days, he had imagined this moment—the two of them alone, the vows behind them, and the rest of their lives stretching out ahead. And yet, he found himself focusing less on what lay ahead and more on the woman before him.

"Come here, wife," he said, his voice gentle but firm.

Her gaze snapped to his, her eyes wide and questioning. He could see her hesitation, and he softened his tone. "Please?"

After a beat, she moved hesitantly toward him. Before she could settle, he reached out and lifted her effortlessly onto his lap. She let out a small gasp, her hands flying to his chest as if to steady herself. He chuckled softly, unable to resist teasing her a little.

"Philip!" she exclaimed, though her tone lacked any real reproach.

"Yes, Annabel?" he replied, his lips curving in a slow smile.

She shifted slightly, her face a delightful shade of pink. "This ... this does not seem proper."

He raised an eyebrow. "You are my wife. I believe that makes it entirely proper."

Her lips parted as if to argue, but no words came. Instead, she looked at him, her expression a mixture of uncertainty and something that looked very much like trust. The realization sent a strange warmth spreading through his chest.

"Are you nervous?" he asked quietly, his tone softening.

She hesitated, then nodded. The vulnerability in the slight gesture made his heart twist.

"Do not be," he murmured, reaching up to brush a loose strand of hair from her face. "You have nothing to fear from me."

Her eyes met his, and the sincerity in her gaze made him feel as though the world had steadied beneath him. "I believe you," she replied softly.

Those three words struck him harder than he expected. He tightened his arms around her slightly, a surge of protectiveness washing over him. She had chosen him, trusted him, despite the whirlwind of circumstances that had brought them together. He would not fail her.

He pressed a kiss to her forehead, letting the simple act speak the words he could not yet say.

"I am glad you are my wife," he declared quietly, his voice rough with emotion he had not intended to reveal.

She blinked up at him, her own expression softening. "And I am grateful for you," she replied, her fingers clutching at his lapels.

For a long moment, they simply looked at each other. Philip felt a profound sense of contentment settle over him. Whatever doubts had plagued him in the days leading up to their wedding faded. This woman, his Annabel, was everything he had not dared to hope for. He would do whatever it took to keep her happy.

He shifted slightly, his arms still around her. "Annabel," he began, his voice low. "I have wanted this moment since the day we met. You must know that I—"

But he stopped himself. She deserved more than rushed declarations in the back of a carriage. There would be time enough for that later. For now, he would let her set the pace.

"Never mind," he said with a small smile. "We will have plenty of time to talk later."

She tilted her head, curiosity flickering in her eyes, but she did not press him. Instead, she rested her head against his shoulder, her trust warming him in a way he had not thought possible.

As the carriage swayed gently, Philip let himself enjoy the moment. Whatever challenges lay ahead, they would face them together. For the first time in years, he allowed himself to believe that the future might hold something more than duty and regret.

But as Annabel's breathing steadied against him, he could not entirely banish the shadow of Richard's earlier words. Secrets had a way of surfacing, no matter how deeply buried. And when they did, he prayed they would not shatter the fragile trust he had built with the woman now nestled in his arms.

CHAPTER TEN

"The beginning is always today."

Mary Shelley's Frankenstein

∽

Their argument started over dinner. After a long day of traveling, both Annabel and Philip were weary by the time the meal was served. The cold ham, braised potatoes, and thyme carrots had been quickly prepared at Philip's request for a simple supper, hoping to ease their arrival at Avonmead.

Both had fallen on their food with the desperation of travelers who had not eaten properly in hours, silence reigning until their initial hunger was satisfied.

"Philip, why have you not spoken with Richard in three years?" Annabel's question cut through the soft clatter of silverware.

Philip froze mid-motion, his fork hovering over his plate. He set it down deliberately, feigning a casual deportment that did not fool her. "My sweet, it is our first night together. Let us not spoil it by discussing Richard. Another time, perhaps?"

"But Richard seemed to think your decision to marry me was related to a dispute between you," she pressed, her tone gentle but insistent.

Philip sighed, his gaze slipping away from hers. "Annabel, Richard is the furthest thing from my mind at present." His voice softened, a teasing note creeping in. "I was just thinking about how we might enjoy our wedding night later this evening."

Annabel shot a mortified look at the footman standing against the far wall, her cheeks warming to a vivid pink. "Philip!" she hissed under her breath, glaring at him.

"My dear, the servants are not fools," he said with a slight smirk. "They are well aware of what newlyweds typically do on their wedding night."

Her blush deepened, and she cast an apologetic glance at the footman, who remained impassive. Undeterred, Annabel returned her attention to Philip. "If it concerns me, or your decision to marry me, I believe I have a right to know what happened."

Philip's expression tightened. "It does not concern you," he said brusquely. Then, clearly attempting to redirect the conversation, he leaned forward, his voice dipping into a warmer tone. "Annabel, I must tell you—you are absolutely radiant in that gown."

Her focus wavered as she glanced down at her attire, the striking saffron silk accented with ivory underskirt and intricate pearl beading. The dress was undoubtedly lovely, but she shook her head, apparently unwilling to let him distract her. "Thank you, but you are changing the subject."

"I am attempting to protect you," he responded quietly, his earlier lightness gone.

"From what?" Her voice was soft, almost fragile, but it struck him like a hammer blow.

Philip leaned back in his chair, crossing his arms. His fatigue was catching up with him, sharpening his frustration. "From matters that are painful and in the past. Why dig into old wounds?"

Annabel met his gaze steadily. "Because I want to understand you, Philip. I thought we were to have a partnership."

He stiffened at her words, and a shadow crossed his very soul. "Some things are best left buried, Annabel."

The rest of the meal passed in tense silence, broken only by polite exchanges with the footman. When the last course was cleared away, Philip stood abruptly, pushing his chair back. "Shall we adjourn to your chambers?" he asked, his tone polite but distant.

Annabel hesitated before nodding.

Reaching her bedchambers, Philip shut the door behind them and turned toward her with a tender expression, but Annabel was not to be distracted. "Philip," she began, her voice almost pleading, "please promise me that your quarrel with Richard has nothing to do with why you married me."

"Annabel, it is our wedding night," he responded, his voice edged with frustration. "Tonight is supposed to be about us—about the vows we took this morning."

Her brow furrowed, her concern evidently deepening. "But how can I trust—"

"Blazes, Annabel!" Philip exploded, his voice rising before he abruptly caught himself. He took a step back, his hands falling to his sides. "The fact that I stand here should be clear why I married you."

Her lip trembled, and she looked away, the hurt in her eyes piercing through his temper. His chest tightened with regret, but his own turmoil held him back. He was a man caught between past and present, his emotions tangled in ways he did not yet know how to explain—or control.

Philip sighed heavily, running a hand through his hair. "Perhaps we are both overly tired," he said, his tone softer now. "Let us rest, Annabel. We can speak tomorrow, with clearer minds."

She stepped aside, creating a path for him to leave. He hesitated before taking her hand and raising it to his lips. "Good night, duchess," he murmured, his voice laden with unresolved emotion.

He exited the room before he could say anything further, closing the door gently behind him. The click of the lock echoed in the hall, a stark punctuation to their fraught conversation.

Alone now, Philip leaned against the other side of the door, his head bowed. Jane's voice rang in his ears, a specter from the past: *"You are a menace, and I do not want you in my chambers again, Your Grace!"* The memory clawed at him, dredging up a wave of shame and sorrow he had tried desperately to bury.

He pushed himself upright with a resigned sigh and strode down the hall. Annabel deserved better than his dark regrets—but he feared he did not know how to give it to her.

∼

Annabel slept poorly; her insides hollowed with disappointment. Her confidence in their marriage was shaken, and she could not think how to bridge the chasm that had formed between her and her new husband. She had had so much hope for their future together, and it seemed founded on her own naïveté and glib misunderstanding of who Philip really was.

Annabel suspected she was being melodramatic, but all felt lost, and she did not know what she could do to restore their convivial interplay. She cried into her pillow, which just made her more miserable and uncomfortable since she had to wipe up her tears, which had dripped down her cheek and streamed down her neck and into her nape. She had to turn the pillow over to rest her head on the dry side. Then switch pillows after she had dampened both sides because it took some time for the tears to flow to a stop.

She tossed and turned all night. Each time she awoke, she remembered their argument and re-experienced the keen loss of affection and closeness until she finally fell into an exhausted sleep at dawn.

It was late morning when she finally awoke. She could see from the light that she had slept later than her usual time, but she did not have the energy to rise. Her heart physically pained her. She wanted to return to the day before, in the carriage, before she had pressed him, when they had shared those magical moments together. It had been a mistake to push him so hard, and she had to admit that she may not have been fully herself. The over-excitement and lost sleep over the past week had compounded and taken its toll.

Last night, she admitted to herself, she *had* been suffering from exhaustion as Philip had pointed out. As a result, she had handled the conversation with drama and impatience. Her poor judgment had ruined her own wedding night, the only one she would ever have.

She heard the door open and listlessly she turned her head on her pillow, expecting to see Mary come to clean her room.

Instead, she found Philip standing inside the room as he shut the door behind him. His clothes were rumpled, and he was barefoot, while his face looked as haunted as she felt, with deep shadows under his eyes. Noticing he had suffered during the night as she had made her feel better. Perhaps it was evidence that he cared about making their marriage work as much as she did. Maybe they were in this together, and he would work to repair it as she wanted to do?

"I am sorry, Annabel." Tears of relief welled in her eyes, and she sat up to receive him. Philip strode across the room urgently. He sat on the edge of the bed and opened his arms. Annabel emitted a low sob as she buried herself in his chest. He wrapped his arms tightly around her. "Can we start again, my beautiful wife?"

Annabel nodded emphatically into his shoulder, her tears drying up. "I want to make this marriage work. I am so sorry for pressing you to talk about it."

"I will tell you about Richard, but not yet. Can you give me a little time? I have been alone with my thoughts for a long time, and I am not accustomed to discussing such subjects. It is embarrassing and painful, but I promise you I will talk to you about it as soon as I am ready." He held her against his broad chest, his long arms engulfing her much smaller body. She could hear his heart beating, and it was the most wonderful sound she had ever heard. He rested his head against her disheveled hair as he clasped her close, and she felt a rush of hope restoring her to her natural state of optimism. They could work together to form a strong marriage if they were both willing participants. Philip's presence was a balm, a vow that they were in this marriage together.

"You promise?"

"I promise. I will always tell you the truth. But sometimes you will have to be patient and give me a little time. I have to get used to the notion that I can bare my thoughts to you. I have placed my faith unwisely in the past, but know this, Annabel, I do trust you. We will build a strong marriage."

Annabel gave a happy sigh as his words mirrored her thoughts of moments ago. This new beginning was important to her.

"You will have your time. Now let me up."

Philip let her go, and she clumsily lifted herself, straightening her maidenly night rail and hopping down from the bed. She made her way over to the washstand where a jug of cold water, some towels, and a washbasin were waiting. She poured some water in and then used a towel to clean her face and water to rinse her mouth. When she felt presentable, she walked back to where Philip sat up against her headboard. He regarded her affectionately and looked up at her standing beside him, arching one of his blond eyebrows in query.

"I am still in my bedroom in my night rail. As far as I am concerned, this still counts as my wedding night."

Philip chuckled, his gray eyes sparkling. "I cannot fault that logic."

CHAPTER
ELEVEN

"The companions of our childhood always possess a certain power over our minds which hardly any later friend can obtain."

Mary Shelley's Frankenstein

∽

The afternoon light shifted slowly across the room as Annabel rolled on her back and rubbed her eyes, groggy from the long hours in Philip's arms. She stretched her body and reached out. Philip's spot on the bed was still warm, indicating she had just missed him arising. She smiled in happiness.

She started when she heard a knock on the door. Then gasped in surprise when the door opened to reveal a familiar, round face peeking around it. Annabel grasped the counterpane and pulled it up to her chin.

"Mrs. Harris!"

"Aye, child. It is me."

"How are you here?"

"Your new husband had a word with Lord Filminster before the two of you left yesterday. The baron was in the pouts. Apparently, my change in position is most inconvenient for him, but he released me last night and I arrived in the second carriage with your trunks. The baron said your husband will pay me an entire quarter's wages on behalf of his lordship for letting me go without notice. And pay me for the quarter I am to work here. I'm to be rich with two quarters' worth of wages!"

The housekeeper made her way into the room bearing a laden tray, which she balanced on the end of the bed.

"His Grace organized this before we even left yesterday?"

"Aye, something about his new bride getting her heart's desire for her wedding day. His lordship complained at length about the duke's ux—uxo—uxorious nature, whatever that means. I am sorry to say that I believe His Grace had to promise the two of you would visit soon to make it up to the baron for my leaving with no notice or replacement to take over my duties."

Annabel winced at the idea of one of the baron's infamous dinners, but quickly brightened and clapped her hands in delight. "I am so happy to see you, Mrs. Harris!" She grew embarrassed a moment later as she realized she was lying under her counterpane and sheets in the afternoon.

"My girl, the duke's home is quite impressive. My new room is larger than I am used to, and there is a beautiful selection of fine silver to care for. I think I shall like it here. Although there is an ill-tempered butler I need to tame downstairs. He seems to think he knows more than me, but I will set him straight directly!"

"Clinton? He seemed most proper to me."

Mrs. Harris snorted in dissent. "More like a proper stick up his bum."

Annabel chuckled at her convivial attendant's unusual display of ill humor. "Mrs. Harris, I don't think you can say that. Besides, I thought he was a discreet man with exemplary composure. What did you do to cause his ire?"

Unexpectedly, the older woman colored with a ruddy blush. "Never you mind, duchess, never you mind. Now, what are your plans for the rest of this afternoon?"

Annabel noted the transparent attempt to change the subject, but let it pass. She had her own embarrassments to cover up, such as the evidence of their wedding night. "Will you request a bath be prepared while I rise?"

"Certainly, my girl. As soon as I set down this tray of tea and pastries that your husband ordered for you. You missed the morning meal. I guess you had better things to do this morning."

Annabel's abashed giggle was out before she could stop it. She shrugged in an attempt at nonchalance as Mrs. Harris brought the tray and set it on the table.

As soon as the door closed behind the housekeeper, Annabel shot out of bed, relieved to find her night rail lying in a heap under the bed, well out of sight. She hurriedly slipped it on and buttoned up before inspecting the room to ensure no more embarrassing details lay on display.

※

ANNABEL WANDERED along wide halls and down staircases until she eventually found her way to the first floor. Once on the main floor, she found she was more familiar with the layout of the palatial manor, and she located the dining room where she and Philip had dined hurriedly the night before. From there she explored the hall, attempting to find the door that led to the servant passages and kitchen. It took a little time roaming up and down, passing the front staircase repeatedly as she tried opening and closing doors. Finally, she stumbled upon a dark corridor behind a discreet, recessed door she thought might lead toward the kitchen, as she could hear the far-off sound of clanging.

As she entered the corridor, voices raised in anger startled her to a standstill. She paused just short of a turn in the hall to take stock.

"It is not how things are done in a *Ducal Household*!" Annabel could hear the capitalization in the loud, injured tones of the husky voice. She was uncertain, but it sounded like it might be Clinton, the butler, engaged in a surprising show of emotion.

"Well, it is how things are done in *This Ducal Household* now that I am the *housekeeper*!"

It nonplussed Annabel to hear Mrs. Harris, and she went racing around the corner, ready to defend her loyal friend against any attack. It amazed her to see both the butler and their new housekeeper flushed with high temper, standing toe to toe. Mrs. Harris's round face stuck up in defiance, her chin squared at the taller man. Clinton looked belligerent, and he started to shout down at her, "Now look here ..."

Both servants froze when they spotted her. Annabel stopped in place as the two older servants jumped apart, one bowing and the other curtsying. "Your Grace ..." they chorused.

"What is happening here?" she demanded. "What are you quarreling about?"

"Quarreling? We have no argument with each other, Your Grace. Just coordinating our day. Can I have some tea brought to you?" The butler seemed, once again, unflappable. It was as if Annabel had imagined the argument she had interrupted, except for the flush receding from his cheeks.

Annabel frowned in confusion as Mrs. Harris stepped forward and ushered her back down the hall. "Come along, Your Grace. We will bring your tea to the drawing room directly. I will show you the way."

Annabel wondered if she was going mad. The two servants were now the height of decorum and acting in unison to bustle her out of the servants' hall. She shook her head in amazement and soon found herself deposited in a purple Trafalgar chair with a plump French stuffed cushion. "Now, see here, Mrs. Harris ..." she protested.

"Time for tea, my girl. I will have it brought presently." The housekeeper bustled out before Annabel could sputter a response, struggling to make sense of the past few moments. The two servants had been engaged in a heated discussion, that was clear, and there had been a strange undercurrent to the interaction she had observed—something she could not quite put her finger on. Perhaps they had a conflict of personalities? But there had been a strange tension to their argument she could not place, yet it reminded her of something.

Besides, she did not want tea. She had just drunk almost an entire pot of Twinings with her very late breakfast.

What on earth had the two been arguing about?

CHAPTER
TWELVE

"My heart was fashioned to be susceptible of love and sympathy, and, when wrenched by misery to vice and hatred, it did not endure the violence of the change without torture such as you cannot even imagine."

Mary Shelley's Frankenstein

∽

"Thank you, *My* Grace." Annabel's hands rested on his shoulders as she pressed a quick kiss to Philip's crown.

He laughed, turning his body to capture her by the waist. Shifting his chair back, he lifted her onto his lap. "Last night was just as enjoyable for me, Annabel."

Her eyes sparkled as she gazed into his eyes, causing his heart to skip a beat as he took in her glowing face. She looked ravishing.

"Not that. For being uxorious and obtaining my favorite housekeeper for me so quickly."

"Faith! Uxorious? I merely considered it a wedding gift, as there was no time to arrange anything."

She chuckled. "The baron's description, not mine. I think it was a lovely surprise. I lo—liked it very much." She looked sheepish, and Philip wondered what she had been about to say.

"Do you plan to continue calling me, *My* Grace?"

"Well, you are a Grace, and you are mine." Philip disguised a shiver of pure pleasure at her affirmative possession of him. He liked … belonging to someone. Nay, he enjoyed belonging to Annabel. She was sweet, assertive, and passionate. Fate was favoring him, and he would grab hold of every moment of enjoyment he could wring from it. He had exited the half-dream world of numbness and private pain he had been living in the past three years, to discover a whole new world of light, colors, and experiences. Overwhelmed, he leaned in to nuzzle her neck, hiding the emotions that must play across his face. How had he secured such a bright light in his empty existence?

"What will you do today?" he queried hoarsely, needing a change of subject to compose himself.

"I will meet the servants properly and ensure Mrs. Harris settles in. If there is time, I shall visit the library and locate all the books I must read to prepare me for my role of duchess. Richard had not planned to take me to London for some time, and I expected to brush up on my Debrett's and etiquette books once we married. However, that was for the mere role of countess; now I have the much more daunting task of duchess to prepare for."

Philip embraced her slight form before lifting her to stand next to him. "That reprobate probably intended to keep you in the country forever, lest you meet his mistresses. I do plan to take you to London in the not distant future, so preparing is an excellent step to take. Will you need help?"

"I think I should read the books with the intention of actually learning and practicing. Admittedly, I was not an attentive student when my governess gave me those types of lessons, since the idea of ever using them was far from my mind. I was far more interested in reading novels and books about travel. I would like to practice on you so that you can let me know if I am applying my manners *and airs correctly*." She said the last with a haughty enunciation and wave of the hand as if an arrogant old biddy receiving an introduction from a social inferior at Almack's.

Philip laughed at her irreverent humor, picturing a young Annabel staring out the window during her lessons. "We can do that. I can also have my man of business hunt down an appropriate tutor or companion to assist you in the finer details. Either way, you are my duchess, and I will be right at your side when we introduce you to society. How about I join you in the library so I can pull the books you need, and then you can meet the servants after that?"

"You will be my hero if you climb the ladders for me."

～

As they entered the enormous library, Annabel felt her head would spin yet again. The dizzying heights of two stories of bookshelves were a sight to be reckoned with, the room lit with bright exterior light from the wall of windows on one end. Small, leaded panes made them appear like a million little squares etched on the rich tapestry of blue sky and trees beyond. Latticed wood on the interior formed Moroccan-inspired arches, and a large, exotic medallion high above overlaid the bank of panes. An unexpected architectural feature, but Annabel vaguely recollected from their tour that one of the Markham ancestors had traveled to Northern Africa to engage in trade negotiations on behalf of the Empire. She could almost imagine the whiff of exotic spices as she gazed up at the intricate work that hinted of far-off lands and travel.

Philip pointed out the different sections of the library so she might find her way around the books.

"Do you have a favorite, Philip?"

"I have been much taken with *Waverley* in recent years."

Annabel nodded. "A tale of the bonds of friendship and honor prevailing over the wars of men."

Philip looked at her with appreciation in his eyes. "I like Edward had a mind of his own."

"It surprises you I have read it. The men in my life have provided poor examples to look up to. I have to read novels to find my mentors."

"Reading broadens the mind. Here at Avonmead, you will have plenty of opportunity to broaden your mind even further."

"Good gracious, I doubt I can make a dent in this gargantuan library. I have never seen so many books in one place."

"You did not tell me what your favorite book is?"

"That is a difficult decision. I love *Pride and Prejudice*, as it is so inspiring, but recently I enjoyed *Frankenstein; or, The Modern Prometheus*, although it was very dark."

"Ah, perhaps the two books should be melded together. *Pride and Prejudice and Monsters*, if you will."

Annabel giggled. "That would be most enjoyable. Perhaps Wickham could secretly be the monster!"

"Indeed. Wickham could steal Lydia away to keep her in a dungeon for Mr. Darcy to rescue," he countered.

Annabel's laugh was full and unapologetic, but faltered as Philip stared down at her with a happy grin spread across his face. Several seconds passed before he spoke. "Wait here, and I will collect the volumes you need."

Philip took to the spiral wooden staircase that led to the second level. He hunted around the shelves, the lower half of his body obscured by the wooden bannisters of the landing that embraced the three walls of books. An edifying moment hit her—as lady of the manor, she now had part ownership of all this magnificence of knowledge. She felt the need to pinch herself to ensure this moment was real.

Soon Philip descended the winding stairs with an armful of books. He set them down on the long desk below the wall of windows and placed the two volumes of Debrett's *Peerage* on the top. "This set is a little out of date, so I will arrange for a newer edition. Fortunately, as my duchess, almost everyone you meet with will be your social inferior, which makes maintaining correct protocols far simpler than the role of countess."

"Nevertheless, I believe I will need to memorize quite a bit. Thank you for assisting me."

"Wife, it is my pleasure," he said as he grabbed her by the waist to embrace her with affection. "Feel free to conduct your studies here in the library. This desk has ample light for a long part of the day, so you may find it the best location for reading. Or that sofa near the window." He pointed out a sumptuous Morocco leather sofa with mahogany framing. "Despite how elegant it looks, it is actually rather comfortable for a prolonged visit in the library."

He settled a quick kiss on her forehead and left the room. Annabel stood staring after him as he reached the carpeted corridor, listening to his muffled steps retreating down the hall as she huffed in pure contentment. Breathing in the smell of aging leather and paper, she took in the brilliant view of the parks behind the manse and the interior two stories of bibliophile heaven. Bouncing in glee, she took up a spot next to the desk at the window to survey the assorted books. Her husband had selected reading befitting a new duchess of the realm.

∼

ANNABEL AND PHILIP were enjoying a lively discussion about correct forms of address. Annabel, who could not make sense of some of the finer points of society etiquette, was arguing over her soup, waving her spoon about to emphasize her reasoning. In her opinion, the rules bordered on the ridiculous and illogical, laden with minute nuances that could get a young woman pinned as a social pariah. Philip had stated his rejoinders based on tradition, and there had been fair points to his arguments.

Over the past week, they had settled into a routine of convivial interaction during the day and honeymoon of sorts in the evening, when they adjourned to bed early. Annabel could live in this paradise for the rest of their days. It was heaven to spar with her clever, witty husband and lie in his powerful arms until he rose at dawn. Memories of her wedding day debacle had faded, and she was slipping into a new life at Avonmead that she much enjoyed.

She had just spooned up her white soup after making, in her mind, a particularly intelligent point when the door burst open. She swung her head around to find a disheveled and heavy breathing Richard dressed in his riding clothes and smelling of spirits and horse. Clinton came up behind him, sweating and panting in pursuit. Out of breath, the ruddy butler swept past him to announce, "The Earl of Saunton," before casting a baleful eye at the offending party. The servant twirled on his heel and departed.

"Halmesbury. Annabel." Richard sneered as he gave a drunken bow.

"What are you doing here, Saunton?"

Richard straightened as a flash of fury crossed his face. "It is beyond the pale, Halmesbury! I have been seething for days since I encountered you at Filminster's. Your arrogant interference is beyond the pale!" he roared, making Annabel jump in her seat at the unexpected rage and volume.

"We will go to my study," said Philip in a low, angry voice. He stood abruptly. His chair teetered for just a moment before righting.

"Does Annabel know why you married her? Does she know about our sodding *imaginary* love triangle? Although now it is a love quadrangle, I suppose."

"Saunton, go to my study," hissed the duke.

"While I think it is high time that Miss Ridley ... I mean, the fine Duchess of Halmesbury be told that she is a sacrificial pawn on the chessboard of your petty rev—*hic*—venge. Shall I tell her, or are you going to be a man and explain why you married her?"

Philip turned to Annabel. "Get out!" he barked. It took her a moment to realize he was barking at *her*, not Richard. A calamity of emotions hit her, slowing her reactions so that all she could do was stare dumbstruck into Philip's face. The dramatic change in his mood was jarring, and the coldness with which he spoke froze her chest in a painful vise-grip.

Philip raised his voice. "GET OUT, ANNABEL!"

"But ..." she spluttered.

"NOW, ANNABEL!"

Her throat thickened and her eyes pricked as she clumsily pushed her chair back, accidentally crashing it onto the floor as she rose in haste. She did her best to gather her dignity, but she was afraid there was nothing graceful about her exit as she stumbled from the room, nearly tripping over her own skirts. Heavy footfalls sounded, and the door slammed hard behind her, shaking the frame and the floor with its force. She stood in the hall in shock, her thoughts unraveling. Her head felt thick, and she couldn't think what she should do next as she pressed a hand to her stressed stomach. She raised the back of her hand against her mouth to muffle a sob, realizing she could not stand in the hall like a ninny, lest the two men exit the room and find her there.

She considered remaining to eavesdrop, but her hands were icy and her breath thready. She did not think she could cope with any revelations that she may overhear if she remained, so she took a tentative step away from the door and then another. It seemed prudent to retreat until she could compose herself, so she continued up the primary staircase, barely aware of her environ until she reached her bedchamber and lay on the bed to stare at the ceiling. Confusion and dismay coalesced into dry sobs that racked her frame. His rage had been so out of character, and she battled to make sense of why Philip had thrown her out. Was her marriage an act of revenge? Richard had implied there was more to Philip's incentives than he had revealed —was it true? What secret was her husband hiding? What did the two men discuss downstairs?

Her hopes of aspiring affection from her husband had seemed a realistic goal over their first few romantic days together, but what did she truly know about her duke and his intentions? Perhaps he made every girl feel special with that intent manner he had of listening carefully to her, as if what she said mattered. As if *she* mattered. What if she was only a pitiful project, such as his foundlings, that he was treating kindly with no true investment of emotion? A pathetic woman in need of saving. Tolerated as a necessary substitute for the woman he had truly loved.

Her thoughts clouded into a storm of tears as she felt her tenuous happiness of the past few days evaporating to ashes in the pit of her stomach.

∽

Philip had not experienced such rage since he had thrown Richard out of Avonmead on his ear the night of his wife's death. The man was a dog, and he wanted him out of his house, far away from his lovely bride.

"Annabel is mine. You have no right to enter my home, you despicable blackguard. I told you the last time you were here to never darken my doorway again."

"Have you?"

"Have I what?" Philip demanded, fury heating his veins.

"Have you told Annabel the true reason you married her? She thinks you are a hero who rescued her from a terrible and fated union with me but, damn it, I really care about her. While you are just playing out some petty revenge as a jealous husband who can't see the truth ... the truth ... for the trees." Richard swayed drunkenly.

"You are not in a fit state, so I will not argue with you over this. Suffice it to say that I care about Annabel far more than you ever could, and you know nothing of my reasons for saving her from *an arrogant reprobate like you*!" Philip had felt a flash of satisfaction at his articulate retort until he noticed that his inebriated cousin had fallen into a dining chair and passed out.

Cursing, he stalked over to ring the bell. Clinton appeared in moments with two hefty footmen, clearly expecting his signal to return and throw the drunken lord out on his ear. Unfortunately, his drunken cousin would have to stay the night. If they attempted to throw Saunton out, he would simply lie in an intoxicated pile on the front drive. *Blast!* He wanted to rid himself of the despised man's presence without delay.

By the time Philip had gotten the earl into a guest chamber for the night, with express instructions to throw his unwanted presence out at the crack of dawn after they had fed him a cup of coffee, his breathing was coming in shallow, infuriated bursts. He paced in his bedchamber, but he was too angry to sleep, and he had no desire for company, or to have Annabel question him on Richard's accusation.

Blast, blast, blast!

He stalked out, banging the door as he exited. Once entrenched in his study, he poured a brandy and drank it down in quick gulps before pouring another. He froze, facing the sideboard when he heard light footsteps enter the room.

"Not tonight, Annabel." He did not turn and continued to stare at his decanter.

He heard her take a deep inhalation as if to say something. The next moment, she exhaled and was gone. Philip was left alone, staring into the shallow depth of his brandy.

He went to sit in the stuffed armchair, to stare at the flames in the fireplace that had not yet been extinguished. His household was in uproar and the fire temporarily forgotten, which suited him fine. It reflected his mood.

CHAPTER THIRTEEN

"I am alone and miserable; man will not associate with me."

Mary Shelley's Frankenstein

~

Philip started from a restless doze, his late wife's pained words blending with Richard's drunken tirades to form a tapestry of unsettling dreams. Dreams where the weight of solitude pressed on him, threatening to pull him into despair.

The room was dim, the onset of evening casting long shadows. Sconces flickered gently, their light spilling across the floor, while the fire in the hearth danced, painting shifting patterns on the walls. A servant must have entered while he slept, tending the room with quiet efficiency.

He lifted his head, his neck protesting from hours spent awkwardly bent against the arm of the chair. Groaning softly, he reached for the decanter on the nearby table and poured a measure of amber liquid. He heard the faint splash of droplets escaping the glass, but he had no energy to ensure the table was spared from the spill. Raising the drink to his lips, he swallowed deeply, seeking to silence the voices of the past that still lingered in the corners of his mind.

∼

It had been three days since Richard had burst into their dinner. Annabel knew it had been precisely three days, as this was the third night she was taking her supper alone in the dining room. She kept hoping Philip would join her, but as the hour ticked slowly by, it was clear he had no such plans. He had retreated into his study when he was not out riding in the park. She had barely caught a glimpse of him, other than a fleeting shadow at the end of a passage.

She had never felt so alone.

A tear slipped down her cheek, and with dull detachment, she watched it fall onto her plate. She wished she knew what was wrong. What had Philip and Richard discussed after she had left the room? Why had her promising new marriage suddenly unraveled into ... into ... into this desolate silence?

Another tear slid down her chin, and she let it fall. She could put on a brave face, but what was the point? There was no one here to notice the effort.

The sound of low footsteps reached her ears, and she immediately felt a flicker of resentment, her earlier instruction to the footmen to leave her undisturbed clearly ignored. Lacking the energy to care, she did not bother to look up as the door clicked shut and a chair scraped the floor beside her.

Mrs. Harris settled heavily into the seat, giving a small huff of exertion.

"What happened, my girl?"

Annabel bit back an uncharitable remark. She could not take her sorrow out on the older woman, who was her only source of comfort in this unfamiliar house. Staring at her plate, she knew Mrs. Harris would not let the matter drop. She sighed and relented.

After a moment, she shrugged. "I do not know. Lord Saunton shouted something about a love triangle—or love quadrangle, or some such nonsense—and then Philip threw me out of the room. He yelled at me. He has not spoken to me since." Her voice trembled as more tears splattered onto her plate. "Perhaps he regrets marrying me?"

Mrs. Harris sighed deeply, her hazel eyes clouded with concern. "Child, I do not believe the duke would have married you if he didn't want to. He strikes me as a man who knows his own mind, and no one belowstairs has said otherwise. I suspect something else is troubling him, and he does not know how to face it. According to the staff, his behavior these past three days is entirely out of character. Whatever this is, it is about him, not you. Do not let your mind trick you into thinking otherwise. Sometimes, men just need time to untangle their thoughts."

Annabel mulled this over. "You think he has a problem he cannot face?"

"I do. Based on my experience, men often struggle to share what's weighing on their minds. It can be hard for them to admit when they are vulnerable or hurting. His Grace appears to be grappling with something heavy, and I doubt he will resolve it alone if he has locked himself in his study for three days."

"But what can I do?"

Mrs. Harris gave her an encouraging smile. "It takes a strong woman to refuse to let such a thing fester. Stop feeling sorry for yourself, my girl, and make that handsome husband of yours talk to you. Remember what your dear mother always said: 'Fortune favors the bold!'"

Annabel hiccuped a small laugh as the housekeeper mimicked her mother's tone. "That is exactly what Mama would say."

Her mother's words reignited a flicker of determination. A sudden surge of optimism shot through her as Annabel pushed back her chair and stood. Raising a triumphant fist in the air, she declared, "*Carpe diem!*"

Mrs. Harris blinked, her expression bemused.

"Seize the day, Mrs. Harris, seize the day!"

Annabel marched through the hallways, her slippered feet tapping on the polished floors. When she reached the study, she flung the door open with a bang and stuck her foot against it to keep it from swinging back in her face. She stood in the doorway, hands on her hips, determination blazing in her eyes.

"Husband, we must talk!"

∽

PHILIP OPENED a bleary eye at the interruption and sighed. "Please leave, Annabel."

He knew he was being unreasonable, but the weight of his memories had him trapped. For three days, he had wrestled with the past, and retreating into solitude had seemed the only way to endure the turmoil. Yet every hour in the study only deepened his despair. He glanced at the decanter, knowing another sip would do nothing to help but feeling too defeated to stop himself.

"No!" Her voice rang with confidence, and Philip turned his head in surprise. Annabel strode across the room with determination, her presence like a breath of fresh air blowing away the suffocating shadows that clung to him.

"When did you last eat?" she demanded, stopping next to his chair and planting her hands on her hips.

Philip blinked at her audacity, then frowned as he searched his mind. "I had coffee this morning. Perhaps some toast."

"Well, there is a perfectly fine meal waiting on the table, and we are going to eat it. Then, you will come upstairs to rest. In the morning, when you are yourself again, you will tell me what is troubling you."

Before he could protest, she grasped his arm with a firm but gentle hand and urged him to stand.

"No arguments, Philip. First food, then rest, and then talking." Her tone left no room for negotiation.

For a moment, he hesitated. Then, seeing the resolve in her gaze, he rose to follow her. As she led him toward the dining table, he felt something shift—a small crack in the darkness that had engulfed him. Her presence was a reminder that he was no longer alone, that he had someone at his side willing to face the shadows with him. He disguised a sigh of relief as his bold, compassionate wife stopped his slide into dark despair, gently guiding him back toward the light.

∾

Dawn stole its way into her room. She nestled close to her large, warm-blooded husband. She already felt better, even though they had yet to talk. Philip's color had returned as she had forced him to dinner, his gray pallor evaporating to reveal his usual robust tones. After a quick dinner, they had come to her bedchamber, where a bath had been prepared. She had undressed him and made him wash. Afterward, he had dried himself and joined her in bed, silently wrapping his arms around her before falling into an exhausted sleep.

She opened her eyes and found Philip's deep gray ones gazing at her in the half-light. The corner of his mouth crooked up in a half-smile.

"Philip, what happened?"

"I think—I think perhaps I was grieving."

"Grieving?"

"So much has happened the past couple of weeks. It kept me preoccupied. But with a new beginning, one has to let go of the past. Richard's visit brought the past into the present, and for a moment I got ... lost. Unexpended grief, I guess. I did not take the opportunity to mourn when Jane died. At the time, I sort of suppressed all that emotion. Except for my anger at Richard, whom I threw out in a holy fit of rage. A couple of maids quit because of it which I could not blame them for."

Annabel was silent for a few minutes, thinking. "When my mother died, I was lost. Luckily, I had Mrs. Harris. She forced me to talk about it. My loss, my worries, my pain. Talking helps. Otherwise, the thoughts get locked in your head, and they can get a little disordered trapped in there. When you say them out loud, it is easier to hear the illogic of your thoughts and make better sense of them."

"Hmm. You make an interesting point. I used to talk to Richard all the time, and I was less lonely back then. When it turned out he had no loyalty, I guess I found myself truly alone. My brother and I are not very close." He hesitated. "I guess you want to know what happened with Jane. And Richard?"

"I believe it is time for you to talk about it, *My* Grace." She threw an impudent grin before continuing. "We tried it your way, and now we need to try it my way, as your way turned you into a belligerent drunk, and I happen to like your grace, not your beastliness." She nestled closer to him. He put his arm around her and pulled her into the side of his body as he half seated himself against her headboard.

Philip sighed, his thick blond lashes fanning his broad cheeks as he searched for words. "I am unsure where to begin ..."

He was silent for several moments before continuing. "Jane was the perfect debutante. Proper, lovely, and sweet. I was in love at almost first sight. She was everything I thought I wanted." He went quiet, his expression bemused as his thoughts returned to the past. "As soon as we married, the trouble started. Our wedding night was ... turbulent."

"How so?" she blurted, then felt sheepish. "Sorry, it is your story."

He looked down at her and pressed a quick peck to her forehead. "She was not prepared for our ... ahem ..." Philip sought the right word. "... relations? Her mother died when she was young, and I do not think she had a Mrs. Harris to talk to her about the wedding night. It was most unpleasant. I upset her greatly, as I mishandled it, being much more experienced than she."

Annabel blushed at the direction of the conversation. Drawing a fortifying breath, she asked the question at the foremost of her mind, the answer that Philip needed to express to let go of his past mistakes. "How did you mishandle it?"

Philip looked away and cleared his throat uncomfortably. "It started with kissing. I thought I was gentle, but I must have been too amorous, which shocked her, and then it was downhill from there, so I stopped that night since it was clear it was too much for her. I tried to have a talk about what to expect, which resulted in her weeping. She thought it all sounded beastly, so I left her alone for about a week until I tried again. I had to coax her over two months until we finally consummated the marriage, at which point she started avoiding me. If I tried to visit her, she threw recriminations at me until I floundered for anything to say. To calm her."

"It sounds like the problem was not you, Philip. There must be history there for your late wife that made her so timid."

"That is what I thought, but I am afraid events unfolded to prove me wrong. I started leaving Jane alone, because she appeared calmer when she was not in my presence. I attempted to bridge our relationship by meeting her at breakfast and being especially gentle in dialogue and whatnot. But after three months, Mrs. Thorne came to me and asked if I knew Jane was with child. I was flabbergasted. She must have conceived the one time we ... engaged ... and had never told me. So I wrote to Saunton and asked him to visit, as I felt I was going out of my mind trying to work out how to save my marriage. I needed to talk to someone to work out some sort of strategy—a tactical plan—to bridge the chasm between us, and he was the only one I could think of. We were close back then."

"That sounds like it would have been a good idea."

"Yes, you would think so. However, it made it worse. Saunton arrived, and we discussed the matter. I assumed that as a renowned rake, he knew much about women of every kind. I thought we came up with a good plan of action where I would court her and perhaps hire a widow as a companion. An experienced woman who would keep her company and give her a better perspective on ... ahem ... marital relations."

"That is actually an inspired idea about the companion—a sort of mother or older sister figure to help guide her and campaign on your behalf. Whose idea was that?"

"Richard's."

Annabel was impressed, despite detesting Richard. "He just rose slightly in my estimation."

"Not when you hear the rest." Philip pulled a face. "I tasked my man of business to find a suitable companion while I renewed my courtship. Richard remained on hand to guide me each step of the way. After three weeks, Jane seemed happier—I thought we were improving—until one night she took ill after dinner. Mrs. Thorne and Mary were taking care of her while we awaited a doctor, but by the early hours of the morning, she had a raging fever and was delirious. The doctor said we could not do much other than feed her liquids and sponge her regularly. We took turns to keep vigil, although I barely left her room even when I could. That is when I discovered Richard's true intent in visiting. The reprobate had not enough women in London. He wanted my beautiful Jane, too!" Philip's voice rose in anger as he recounted. Stopping, he clearly struggled to collect himself. "She started crying out for Richard."

Annabel stilled in horror. "You mean ..."

"Yes, they had clearly started an affair during his visit. So you see, it was not marital relations she could not abide, it was me." Philip's face displayed a strange mingle of anger, grief, and shame. "My sweet wife thought I was a beast. She would not stop calling for Richard, crying out how she needed him, loved him, that he could not leave her alone. For hours, I tried to calm her in her delirium while she called repeatedly for another man. Finally, I had Mrs. Thorne seek Saunton out to summon him to the room. Anything to calm Jane down. We met outside this room in the hall, and I told him I knew of the affair and that Jane needed him. The cad denied everything and refused to enter the room. Eventually I returned and pretended I was Richard, taking her hand and comforting her that I was there, and I would not leave her."

"Oh, Philip! I am so sorry." Annabel's eyes moistened at the pain in her husband's voice. She wanted to tell him to stop his recounting, as it was too painful to bear, but she could not. Philip needed to relate it, and she could not display the depths of selfishness that Saunton had. She must permit the duke to finish his story if he was to achieve relief.

Philip shut his eyes tightly, a lone tear still escaping down his cheek to drip off his chin. "I felt so betrayed, but there was no time to have any feelings about it. My wife was gravely ill. I had to be by her side. It only took another day, with Mrs. Thorne and I doing our best to ease her before she expired. My sweet, darling wife who hated me so, and our unborn child. Both gone before I ever formed a meaningful relationship with her. That is when the rage hit me. I hunted Saunton down—he was still here—and I threw his treacherous behind out. He lied the entire time, protesting that he would never touch the wife of such a close friend. I could still hear Jane calling for him over and over again in my mind while he refused to help. I threw him out the door and told him to never darken my doorstep again."

Annabel ran a soothing hand over Philip's chest as he

trembled with repressed emotion. "I am so sorry, husband. You suffered far worse at Richard's hands than I."

Philip's eyes were sightless as he gazed into the past, his mind still lost in the mists of time. He took his time responding. "Thank you for giving me a chance to talk. Do you mind if I go for a ride? I need to clear my mind."

Annabel nodded and slowly rolled away. Philip stood and gathered up his clothes from the night before, exiting through their connecting door.

Annabel looked around her luxurious duchess chambers, filled with warm ivories, rich mahoganies, and splashes of deep red, imagining the beautiful former duchess isolated in these same chambers to avoid her lovelorn duke. Philip's true love. Her heart sank as she quietly accepted that Philip had, indeed, married Annabel in an act of revenge. She had suspected such since their wedding day, but hearing it confirmed was ... depressing.

She brooded on what she would do next. She had chosen the hand she had been dealt, choosing this life with Philip rather than a loveless marriage with Richard as the female equivalent of a cuckold. Was there even a word for a woman who was cuckolded, considering the social norms her father claimed existed for men of Richard's station? Perhaps the word for a female cuckold was simply ... wife? Or, without a doubt, *Richard's wife*.

She admitted to herself that she was lost. How was she to guide her marriage into the happy future she had envisioned? She had chosen this path, and she needed to make the best of it. Philip's experiences were heartbreaking, but now it was time to pick up all of these pieces of life they had and build with them. Being someone's incarnation of revenge was better than being someone's cuckold ... was it not? She needed to be careful to not pin too many hopes or expectations on her husband. His past clearly haunted him, and he still suffered from the loss of his great love.

She would need to devise a plan for their marriage while not becoming too invested in the outcome, lest she be horribly disappointed. She could not afford another stab to the heart, such as the devastating moment she had discovered Richard in the stables. Despondent, she sat up to peer sightlessly in the direction of the window, lost in a gray interior world of thought.

Was she doomed to never be loved? Did she just not have that quality or beauty that would attract a man's unfailing adoration? Perhaps the baron was correct about her. Perhaps she was not as unique as Mama had always claimed, but rather, she was just odd. Not to mention small-minded, to be stricken with jealousy of a tragic dead woman.

∼

ANNABEL HAD FINALLY MADE it back to the library. She had not seen Philip since he had gone riding that morning. Settling into her role as duchess seemed daunting, but with Mrs. Harris excelling in her duties, Annabel resolved to begin her own training in earnest. She picked up a red leather-bound volume of Debrett's Peerage, trying to ignore the uneasy thoughts that Philip's revelations about his late wife had stirred. Perhaps understanding the past could help her navigate the future.

She was still absorbed in her thoughts when she heard soft footfalls behind her. A familiar pair of arms encircled her gently. Startled, she jumped slightly, but then relaxed as Philip rested his chin on the top of her head.

"Hello, wife," he murmured warmly.

Annabel turned to face him, her heart lifting at his affectionate tone. His windswept appearance and bright eyes gave him an invigorated look she had not seen before.

"Hello, My Grace," she replied, smiling up at him.

"What are you up to, duchess?"

"Spending time with you, I hope," she answered lightly.

A wide smile spread across his face. Taking her hand, he coaxed her to stand. Without a word, he wrapped his arms around her and kissed her, the tenderness in his touch sending warmth through her body.

He led her to the Grecian library sofa and seated her gently before lowering himself beside her. His expression was thoughtful as he gazed into her eyes, his hands encasing hers.

"I have missed you," he confessed softly.

Annabel's chest swelled with emotion. "I missed you too."

He raised a hand to caress her cheek, his thumb brushing lightly across her skin. "These past few days have been a storm in my mind, but you bring the calm."

Touched by his words, she leaned into his hand, closing her eyes briefly before meeting his gaze. Slowly, he leaned in, capturing her lips with his. The kiss was tender but intense as he poured his emotions into the embrace.

They parted, their foreheads resting together. "Philip," she whispered, "I want to build something good with you, but we must talk more, share more."

His gray eyes softened, and he nodded. "We will. I promise."

He pulled her into a close embrace, holding her against his chest. The rhythmic beat of his heart was steady and reassuring. Annabel felt hope blooming within her. They could build a life together, one step at a time, leaving the shadows of the past behind.

There was a future for them—a future of trust, understanding, and perhaps, love. Annabel's spirits soared. They could build a future of their own creation. She thought, just maybe, they could one day share a marriage of love rather than revenge. They could make this work ... as long as Richard stayed away.

CHAPTER
FOURTEEN

"The magnificent appearances of things are delightful to me."

Mary Shelley's Frankenstein

∼

Annabel moved around the guest chamber at Baydon Hall, nervously straightening items in the room as Philip tied his cravat in front of the mirror. He was surprisingly adept, even without his valet to tie the intricate knot of his white silk. He looked dashing in his evening black coat and trousers, although Annabel thought he looked out of character without his customary buckskins and navy or forest green riding coats.

"I can't believe what the baron has done," she repeated, agitated as she paced around the bedchamber and straightened again that which she had already straightened.

"It is fine, Annabel. We promised that we would have dinner with him as reparation for releasing Mrs. Harris to our household. We should have expected he would invite what appears to be the entire local Baydon and Filminster gentry to meet *his* new duke."

"We?" She startled even herself with her high-pitched squeak.

"*I*, then, *I* promised him."

"It looks like he has a minimum of fifty guests for a *family dinner*? This is ridiculous. I cannot believe we had to come here *and* stay overnight."

"We're lucky it is only overnight and that he did not hold an entire ball," Philip said in a placating tone. "Come here so I can button your dress."

She waved a hand impatiently. "Mary can do it." Mary, the servant she had met on her midnight escapade the month before, was now formally her lady's maid. It turned out that the redhead was a sorceress at all preparations, including the ability to tame Annabel's wayward hair, which was excellent because Annabel was decidedly not an expert at it.

"Annabel," he commanded.

"Very well." She stalked over to him, glaring at his elegant reflection in the mirror while he helped her to button up the back of her dress. He had already tightened and tied her stays earlier, sparking an irrational flare of jealousy as she wondered how he had come to be so proficient at dressing a woman. More like proficient at *undressing* a woman, she thought to herself sourly.

"We will both be fine. There is no one of consequence coming tonight, so you can practice being my duchess in public with no pressure or dire consequences. You are superior in rank to all the guests, so you just behave like you are better than them, and there is little chance of addressing them incorrectly as they all must be introduced to *you*. It is pure practice at acting superior. A privilege of your new rank."

Annabel couldn't stop her lips from quirking into a twisted smile. "When you put it that way, it all sounds rather simple."

"It is, and in the morning, we get to leave and return to Avonmead."

Annabel sighed in relief. She moved her gaze in the mirror to view her attire. It was the ivory and saffron dress she had worn for her wedding night supper. She loved the dress, and she wanted to change its fortune by wearing it without associating it with arguing with her handsome husband. She was giving it another chance. It looked wonderful, bringing out golden highlights in her hair and eyes while warming her skin tone. It was not fashionable to have such a skin tone, but she still felt like a duchess with the intricate pearl beads sewn into the bodice, along the line on her sleeve, and down the front seams of the saffron overskirt. "Let us go to dinner, *My* Grace."

Philip's eyes creased as he smiled at her in the mirror. "That is the spirit, sweet."

⁓

THE CONFRONTATION with the baron occurred after dinner, when the men had gone to the billiard room to enjoy brandy and cigars. Philip was not fond of strong spirits under normal circumstances, so he sipped his brandy sparingly while declining a cigar with the wave of a hand. One privilege of rank was that he did not have to comply with social mores such as filling his lungs with foul cigar smoke, and no one could question his choices.

Filminster called across the room to get his attention. Philip still had difficulty reconciling the idea that the vile little man had sired a lively, beautiful woman such as Annabel. He could only think that the late baroness must have been an incredible lady. The baron blustered with fellow decrepit toadies of the local gentry near a grand fireplace, his attitude growing increasingly bombastic throughout dinner, while the brandy the older man consumed with excessive vigor was not making him any easier to bear. Philip pretended he did not notice the man beckoning him over while he continued his discussion with the local doctor, who was an erudite, bespectacled man of his own age, and quite pleasant company.

"Son!" the baron bellowed a second time. Philip bit back his annoyance.

"If you will excuse me, doctor?"

His studious companion gave a polite bow. "Of course, Your Grace."

Philip wound around the billiard table, avoiding a cue that suddenly thrust out in his path when he passed too close to the players. He reached the fireplace where Filminster and his cronies clustered around him, looking like a coven of spindly male witches with their stooped shoulders and pot bellies draped in elegant attire. Philip's keen eye could make out chest and thigh padding, and he had to catch himself from shaking his head in disgust at the poser dandies out in the country trying to pretend they were the height of London sophistication. Filminster certainly knew how to pick birds of a feather.

"Filminster," he greeted.

"Papa to you, Halmesbury." Philip fought to keep his hand down at his side so he would not slap the obsequious man across the face. Thunder 'n turf, he could not wait to rejoin his wife!

The baron's eyes were glassy with drink as he continued talking. Philip made an effort to pay attention. "I was just telling my friends here how you bargained for that flibbertigibbet daughter of mine as if she were a prize thoroughbred at Tattersall's, rather than the hoyden we all know her to be here in Baydon."

Fiery anger rose through Philip's chest, and he was pretty certain his ears had turned a deep red as he struggled to hold his temper under control.

∼

ANNABEL HAD LEFT the stuffy drawing room through the terrace doors. The gossiping women of the baron's circle had quickly grown tiresome. The whole evening had been tiresome from the outset. She wished she had known to expect such a large gathering of Filminster's favorite people so she could have prepared herself to meet them. These were the local gentry whom Filminster loved mostly because he was superior in rank to all of them, which meant they all sallied up to him with sycophantic fawning that the baron loved. How her mother and he had coexisted in a marriage, begetting not one but two children, she could not work out. Lady Filminster had been a wonderful, down-to-earth woman who found every person she met worthy of her interest. The opposite of Lord Filminster's vanity.

She was hovering outside the open windows of the billiard room, but was planning on leaving because of the nauseating cigar smoke wafting through the window, when she heard him. She had only heard her husband raise his voice once before, the night Richard had barged in on their intimate supper. He had mentioned losing his temper with Richard when Jane had died, but other than that, she would have staked her life on the fact that the duke was the epitome of social manners, a beacon of etiquette and good breeding.

"Filminster, you blustering buffoon! That is my duchess you just disrespected!" Philip roared so loudly that the windows seemed to shake with the force of it. He must have calmed himself, as his voice had dropped a couple of octaves when he spoke next, but the anger was still evident in his loud umbrage. "Her Grace is a diamond, and it is your loss to not enjoy her exquisite charms. It is my mistake to bring her here. A classic case of 'cast not your pearls amongst swine.' I am taking my lovely wife home to where she is appreciated."

A door banged loudly. Philip must have stormed from the room. Annabel stood with her clenched fist pressed against her mouth in wonderment. She could not deny in that moment that she loved what Philip had just done. Nay, she loved *him*. He was magnificent, springing to her defense. Her chest heaving with excitement, she raced back to the drawing room and entered from the terrace as Philip entered from the hall and swung his head around, looking for her in the large room. Spotting her, he strode over, raised her hand, and placed a gentle kiss on her gloved fingers, spreading warm tingles up her arm. "Shall we go home, wife?"

She grinned from ear to ear, elated at his consideration. "Someone once told me that there were fates worse than death awaiting overnight riders."

"I shall arm the footmen and coachman and tell him to drive like the wind. Like the very hounds of hell are chasing us. It is excellent weather with a full moon, and I think my wife deserves to sleep in her own bed," he whispered, so curious onlookers in their colorful evening dresses could not overhear. "I will inform the men and meet you upstairs to change."

"What of the baron?"

"What of him? You can see him if you like, or you cannot see him. The choice is yours but, for tonight, he no longer has the pleasure of your company."

"Well, My Grace, that all sounds lovely. However, the baron's world is uncommonly small, and these people's cloying admiration is enormously important to him. So, you are going to have to go back in there with the men and make a ribald remark about newlywed men being cranky from lack of sleep and make some sort of public apology to restore his credibility with them."

Philip groaned. "Stuff! Please do not ask me to do that!"

"It will be fine. You are a duke, so they will just assume you are eccentric. But pull my father aside and—privately, as you should have done—inform him you will tolerate no more disrespect to me."

"He will decide for sure that I am an uxorious husband."

"Not uxorious, duke, just a good man who is going to feel guilty if he does not repair this now. The baron is a weak man. The embarrassment will have too much impact on his self-esteem. It has extra force when a set down comes from a man as important as you. I appreciate the stand you made, but we cannot leave him publicly humiliated. I doubt he will ever have the bravado to insult me in your presence again after what just happened."

"How do you know what just happened?"

She threw him an unrepentant smile. "I was hoping to

beckon you into the gardens, so I happened to be listening at the window."

Philip's gaze swept over her face before he gave a defeated sigh. "I am doing this for you, not him. He is your family, so it is your right to dictate how we deal with him … within reason."

Annabel beamed in elation. Her husband cared about her. Deeply, from all appearances.

∼

As their well-sprung carriage flew through the morning light, Annabel had time to take stock of the revelation that she had fallen in love with her wonderful, heroic husband, who rescued children and stood up for her honor.

It was inevitable. She may have fallen in love with him that very first day when he had courted her with his proposal. The duke was so deserving of love. He did much for his tenants, his local community, and even the great town of Halmesbury.

How could she not adore such a man? A husband who honored his commitments and stayed true to his marriage vows. A husband made miserable by a failing marriage who had fought to win his late wife, staying at her bedside to comfort her while she pleaded for another man. And pretending to be that other man in her last hours on this earth as a mercy on her deathbed.

She loved Philip with all her heart, all his strengths and his weaknesses, and she wanted to be his true wife—to comfort him when he needed mercy, to admire him in his fortitude, to witness his achievements and contribute to his success. Pure devotion coursed through her body. It elated her to be near the one she loved most.

"What?"

She tilted her head at him, puzzled.

"You have been staring at me since we left Baydon Hall. It has been almost an hour," Philip grumbled.

"I was just thinking about how wonderful you are."

Philip seemed to be embarrassed by her praise, looking away. "I am just me."

"And you are magnificent."

He seemed agitated at receiving her admiration, squirming in his seat. "Are you glad we are headed home?" His attempt to change the conversation was transparent.

"Oh, no, My Grace, we will talk for a moment about how much I appreciate you. Thank you for putting the baron in his place. And for restoring his pride after."

"There is an intelligent young doctor from Filminster who will never respect me again after witnessing me make an utter cake of myself. Twice." Philip rubbed his face at recalling the appalling night before. "As we are on the subject, why do you always call him *the baron*?"

It was Annabel's turn to feel nervous as she looked away out the sunlit window at the passing hedgerows. Philip had shared his pain with her in the recent past. She supposed she owed him an answer.

"I do not think of him as my father. When I was little, I spent my time with my mother, who was wonderful and taught me all kinds of things. She was a voracious reader, and she knew about many interesting subjects. She taught me some Latin, read me romantic poetry, educated me on subjects that girls should never be taught. When she died ... when she died, I felt the world had ended. That is when Mrs. Harris took me under her wing. I would follow her around on her duties, and she taught me practical things to fill my time and prevent me from brooding. The baron ... my father … he had no time for me. Weeks or months would pass where I would hardly glimpse him, despite living in the same home. When I was sixteen, he deemed me old enough to join him at the dinner table instead of taking meals in my room. I did not take meals in my room, though. I took them in the kitchen with the servants. Mrs. Harris made them accept me belowstairs. But, lucky me, I got to join the baron when I was sixteen, at which point he would mock me about my appearance, my manner of speaking, anything in which I differed from him. The constant belittling did little for my confidence. How my parents ended up married is a mystery for the ages. I will probably never know what brought them together. This past month with you, I felt my self-confidence growing, now that I am no longer living under his influence." Annabel exhaled. "Until now, I have felt more connected to the servants and the tenants than to the baron, if I tell the truth. I hope hearing that is not disappointing to you, considering I am to fulfill the role of your duchess?"

"Sweet, you are going to be a great duchess. They will publish stories about you, and legends will form around your future escapades. You are beautiful, strong, and intelligent. You can do anything you set your mind to, including mastering silly rules of address, precedent, and etiquette. I am not worried in the slightest."

She beamed back at him. "There you go, being wonderful."

"Come here, my sweet."

Annabel joined him on his bench, burrowing into his side as he put his arm around her to tuck her against his warm body. She rested her head on his hard chest with a contented sigh. As her lids grew heavy from the long evening, short duration of sleep, and early morning departure, she realized it was all going to work out. She would have the marriage she had dreamed of if they kept growing together this way. It was inevitable. It had to be, because her heart was wholly devoted to Philip now and she did not know how to turn back. He would grow to love her over time—to believe otherwise was too devastating to consider.

CHAPTER
FIFTEEN

"How dangerous is the acquirement of knowledge and how much happier that man is who believes his native town to be the world, than he who aspires to become greater than his nature will allow."

Mary Shelley's Frankenstein

∿

The following day found Annabel in the library. She had read and reread the entry in the old copy of Debrett's again and again. An hour must have passed with her eyes glued to the page in front of her. She was struggling to comprehend the words she read, a bedlam of implications unfurling in every direction as her mind tried to come to terms with the information.

She had just begun to read Debrett's from the beginning, quite amused at first how the publisher of the venerated texts had not seen fit to update their printing plates;

the antiquated text used old typefaces with 'f' sprinkled throughout to stand in for the soft 's' sounds.

About fifty pages into the first volume, she had stumbled upon an entry that she wished she could now unread. She had a terrible feeling of disquiet as she stared at the entry and wished she, indeed, had the ability to return in time and go for that walk she had considered earlier in the morning rather than having chosen to read in the library.

Annabel tried to push her uneasiness aside, but it pushed right back and refused to be ignored. If Philip had married her out of revenge, how would he feel when he discovered there may not have been any revenge to take? How would it change the dynamics of their fledgling marriage if he knew Richard was innocent of the allegations that he had flung at his cousin three years earlier?

Annabel read the entry again.

EDWARD MARLEY, Earl of ROWBRIDGE, and Viscount of MARLEY ... by whom he had iffue 1.—Richard, Viscount Marley, born March 27, 1796 2.—Jane, born March 27, 1796 ...

The key part of the entry that Annabel was having difficulty assimilating was that Jane Marley ... was a twin? And her brother's name was ... Richard? Annabel recollected Philip's account of his late wife's illness and death. Could the duchess have been calling for her twin in her state of delirium? But, if that was the case, would Philip not be aware that Jane could have been calling for Richard Marley and not Richard Balfour?

Stuff! This cannot be possible!
Where was this Richard Marley?

Why had Philip not factored the brother into the events that unfolded?

Annabel leafed through the volume to the front page, desperate for an explanation.

Just how old was this copy of Debrett's?

1802?

Why was she reading a copy of Debrett's that was sixteen years out of date?

What had happened to Richard Marley?

If Saunton had not betrayed Philip, what did this mean for her marriage?

Annabel stood in a flurry of skirts, almost upsetting the pile of books stacked on the long desk. She needed to clear her head. It felt like her entire life—her very hope of future happiness—was evaporating. It was time for a brisk walk.

∽

THE WALK HAD FAILED to calm her nerves as much as she had hoped. She stood in the corridor wringing her hands, working up her courage. Squaring her shoulders, she pasted on what she hoped was a relaxed smile and walked up to the study door.

"Philip?"

Philip looked up from his work. Sunlight lit his hair into a glorious crown of blond flames, and he appeared bemused as he smiled at her. "Yes, sweet? Are you recovered from all our travel over the last few days?"

"Yes, I am most glad to be home." Annabel winced in her head while keeping the smile pasted on. *Bosh, most glad?* "I was wondering if you had ordered a more recent edition of Debrett's *Peerage*? It's just that ... the copy in the library ...

it was published in 1802 ..." Annabel was afraid she was mumbling in her attempt to be nonchalant.

Philip looked thoughtful, his mind still on his work, she imagined. "I think we have received a delivery of books. Clinton mentioned something about a crate from Hatchards, which is where my man of business usually fulfills my requests, so it could very well be in that crate. Shall I locate it for you?"

Annabel shook her head. "No need. I will find Clinton to arrange for the books to be brought to the library. I was ..." She stopped, uncertain how to continue.

"Yes?"

"I wanted to thank you for patching things up with the baron. Family ties are important. One has to do one's best to maintain them, even when said family member is a trial," she quipped, doing her best to appear relaxed. "Do you maintain any acquaintanceship with your late wife's family?"

"The late duchess? No. Her father was not close with her. We occasionally see each other at Westminster or one of our London clubs and share a drink, but not much more than that. Her mother passed away young, and the earl's heir presumptive is—was—is her uncle. It was her aunt and uncle who hosted her for the Season when I met her, and I am not aware of any other family members other than their young children, whom I never met. I probably know the uncle better than her father."

"So, no other immediate family?"

"Not that I am aware. As I mentioned, she was rather unworldly, having spent most of her time away at a tiny finishing school somewhere up north. Why do you ask?"

Annabel shifted from foot to foot before repressing any further visible agitation. "Oh, the situation with the baron just made me think of family and the ties that bind us. I wondered if you had any ties that I should be aware of, as I do my duchess studies."

He laughed. "Duchess studies, I like that. And, no, the only ties you need to worry about are my brother and avoiding my dear cousin, Richard. There is Richard's brother to think of, I guess. Have you met Peregrine Balfour?"

She shook her head. It was her understanding that Perry was a rake, as the late Earl of Saunton had been reputed to be. The Saunton apples had not fallen far from that tree, apparently. "As far as I know, Perry does not deign to visit the country. Since the baron has never allowed me out of the county, our paths have never crossed."

"Yes, well, you may not be missing much. Perry is a skirt-chaser of some renown and grim company to boot. Richard is by far the more charming of the two. I find the Honorable Mr. Peregrine Balfour too arrogant for my taste. And I doubt he will ever settle down, since he has no heir to concern himself with while living for the pleasures of the moment, so no family responsibilities to worry about. Shall we take a ride together later today? I need to clear my head once I have completed this work."

Annabel nodded, and they made plans, but her mind was racing with other thoughts. Philip did not appear to be aware of Lord Richard Marley, and he had mentioned the Earl of Rowbridge's younger brother was the heir. She was frightened, restraining herself from wiping her sweating palms, lest Philip notice her distress.

What would happen to *them* if he learned of Richard Marley and discovered he had made a mistake accusing Richard Balfour?

Annabel sat at the library desk, staring out the windows at the afternoon sky. She wished she was out there riding in the parklands with her handsome husband rather than sitting here with the most recent edition of Debrett's *Peerage* open before her. Apparently, they had updated their typefaces since the earlier edition she had studied. As she had suspected, she had found the entry she knew she would find.

> EDWARD MARLEY, Earl of ROWBRIDGE, and Viscount of MARLEY ... *by whom he had issue 1.—Richard, born March 27, 1796, and died May 15, 1806. 2.—Jane, born March 27, 1796, and died October 9, 1815* ...

Jane and her twin would have been only ten years old when the young boy died. It was probable that they had been close, as their mother had passed in 1803, and Philip had mentioned the earl had not spent time with his daughter. Being ill and delirious, the late duchess could well have pleaded for the one person she had shared a genuine bond with. Her brother and twin, Richard Marley.

Annabel dropped her head into her folded arms, feeling wretched, but quickly straightened when she heard Mary arrive with the tea tray. She watched the maid cross the room toward her, with her impressive mane of deep red hair tamed into a tight coiffure at the base of her skull.

"Mary?"

"Yes, Your Grace?"

"How long did you serve in the Marley household?"

Mary looked uneasy as she hesitated, placing the tea tray down on the long desk Annabel had made her own. "I started when I was twelve and then came with Her Grace when she married. About thirteen years, I guess."

"You knew her when she was a child?"

Mary cleared her throat, her eyes darting away. "Hmm," she assented.

"You were there when Lord Richard Marley died?"

The woman flinched and paled, her eyes tearing. "Y-yes," she mumbled.

"How did he die?"

"H-he fell from a tree when he climbed too high and the branch broke. It was … tragic. Lady Jane, I mean Her Grace, was devastated. She cried for months and often woke up screaming for him in the night. It was heartbreaking. She experienced so much tragedy. I-I wish she could have found her happiness. His Grace is a kind man, but I don't think he had enough time to h-help her before she fell ill. I do not think she had the will to live. She became a sad and lonely girl—quite timid after the accident in the orchard. It was like her light had left her."

Annabel felt her own eyes well up in response. "I am glad you were here for her."

"Thank you, Your Grace. I did my best to comfort her, but our difference in stations made it difficult."

Drawing on her resolve, Annabel asked the question that must be asked. The maid would be unhappy, but the information was too important to not press the issue. "Mary, His Grace does not seem to be aware of Lord Richard. Why would that be?"

Mary's face tensed in distress, her blue eyes darting nervously.

"Mary, I would not ask if it was not important. Please, I need to understand."

"The-the earl was devastated by the loss of his heir. He

—he ordered all signs of mourning to be removed and forbade the mention of the little lord, even removing all his belongings and instructing the gardeners to burn it all. A servant was dismissed for mentioning the young lord, and ... Lady Jane was locked in her room for three days with only bread and water after she asked where her brother was, because she was not present at his accident. Her nanny had to comfort her and keep her night terrors a secret. I only know of her troubles because I would watch the young lady on Nanny's days off, and she warned me to hide Lady Jane's grieving from his lordship. People react in different ways to loss, but it was not—it was not a healthy situation because she was not permitted to mourn or talk about it. Within weeks, it was as if the young master had never existed, except in Her Grace's nightmares."

Annabel fell silent, brooding as she thought about what her own life would have been like if the baron had not simply ignored her after her mother's death—if she had not had Mrs. Harris, Brendan, and even Richard to comfort her during her own period of loss as a young girl. Her heart fluttered in compassion for the tragic late duchess. The circumstances that Mary described were not healthy, for there had been no healing if there was no acknowledgment of the Marley family's loss. Instead, the grief must have festered, encysted deep within the late duchess's soul.

After several moments of silence, Mary took her opportunity to hastily depart the room.

What should Annabel do with this information? She was now certain it explained the events of three years prior. It had a bearing on their current circumstances. How would Philip react if he learned Richard Balfour had been innocent of the accusations heaped on him?

Bosh—innocent of these particular accusations, at least.

Richard did not deserve her regard, so she did not owe *him* the truth. Philip did deserve her regard, but this information might ruin the fledgling marriage they were building.

Surely Philip would regret his choice of wife when he knew he had chosen her in error to hit back at his cousin, who was guiltless of this particular wrongdoing. And Philip had been so cheerful since the morning he had shared the pain of his past. He was more relaxed; he smiled more readily. Did it serve any purpose to dredge up the past or lay new guilt about snubbing his closest friend?

All her questions were causing Annabel's head to ache. Best she forget what she had learned for now. She could sort this out once her thoughts were clearer.

∽

PHILIP WAS MAKING his way down the hall to the library when he heard raised voices coming from the servants' passage near the dining room. He stopped in consternation and looked back. The door stood cracked open like someone had intended to close it, but it had failed to latch. Curious, he wandered closer to the door.

He could make out the hoarse voice of his butler, Clinton.

"You harridan, I will never understand how the duke consented to have a termagant like you working in this household!"

"I don't know what a termagant is, but I can't think why someone wonderful such as the duke would have such a stuffed shirt running his household!"

"Shrew!"

"Prig!"

Philip frowned in confusion. It appeared his senior servants did not get along. He considered entering to demand an explanation when a thought occurred to him.

"I will inform the duke of your lax attitude to your duties. One can only hope he will reach the conclusion that a new housekeeper is the only solution. I have seen no one handling the silver in that manner!"

"Then you have seen no one handle silver correctly until you had the privilege of my presence, you old dog." The housekeeper's voice was low but menacing.

His suspicions confirmed, Philip gently shut the door and left the two alone to their contentions. He shook his head in amusement as he continued his search for Annabel, who he was certain would be in the library.

CHAPTER
SIXTEEN

"Seek happiness in tranquility and avoid ambition."

Mary Shelley's Frankenstein

∽

The two weeks since the dinner at Baydon Hall had flown past as she and Philip settled into a routine. In the mornings, they would ride together as he showed her parts of the estate and introduced her to the tenants. Once they returned, he would work in his study while she studied in the library. The more etiquette she studied, the more she discovered she needed to learn about correct behavior. Rules in the countryside, so far from urban London, were not as strict, and she was terrified of embarrassing the duke.

They would come together again at dinner time and discuss lively matters over their repast before Annabel would make her way upstairs. An hour later, once she had bathed and Mary had helped her undress and prepare her nightclothes, Philip would knock on the connecting door to his chamber and Annabel would do her best to not blurt out her growing love for him. At dawn, Philip would slip from her bed and another day would begin.

It was glorious, wonderful, and torturous. She longed to share her feelings—to tell him how happy she was here with him, how she had almost everything she could ever want when she was in his arms, but she knew he could not possibly feel the same, and it would ruin everything to pressure him with unwanted sentiments. So, she bit her lip and embraced him lovingly, expressing her deep regard without words.

She spent more and more time in the orangery that the duke had shown her the day after they returned from Filminster. She had never fancied citrus, but for some reason she had come to love the windowed room filled with the fragrance of oranges and lush foliage on the scaffolding.

She peeled an orange as Philip drank tea across from her, enjoying the morning birdsong they could hear in the trees beyond the orangery. It was blissful sitting with Philip while he read the papers delivered from London.

Annabel watched as Philip turned a page and froze, evidently engrossed in a story. After a few minutes, he looked up to gaze out at the parklands visible through the panoramic windows.

~

Philip cleared his throat and looked at Annabel, who was taking a bite of an orange segment. His gaze lingered on her lips for a moment which glistened with the hint of orange juices on her lower lip.

"Annabel, when did you last see your brother? Brendan,

that is?" Philip withheld a wince. As if she had another brother.

Annabel froze, then chewed in silence before taking a deep swallow. Her expression was tense as she dropped her head to stare at her hands. "It has been four years come Christmastime. Why do you ask?"

"You mentioned that once, but I know little of your brother, and you never mention him." Philip was concerned as her eyes appeared to be glistening.

"I have not seen him since I was fifteen. He had a meeting with the baron just before Christmastime. When he came out, I asked him to go riding with me. He told me he did not have time to spend with silly chits and to get out of his way. I ran off into the park, and when I returned home, Mrs. Harris informed me that Brendan had packed his trunks and left in the family carriage."

Philip remained silent. Finally, he reached over to lift her chin with his large but gentle hand. "And then what happened, Annabel?"

Her brandy eyes were gleaming with unshed tears. Philip felt pangs of empathy that made him want to stop his line of questioning, but he sensed that, as Annabel had forced him to talk about his past, she needed to unburden herself.

"I waited for weeks for his return. Christmastime was always very important to my mother, and after she passed, Brendan and I would honor all of her holiday rituals, so I was sure he would come home for Christmas. I waited right through until Christmas dinner, which was when I realized …" She stopped, chewing on her lip.

"Realized?"

"He would not come home to see me. The holidays were nearly done, and he was enjoying himself somewhere without me. It was like losing my mother all over again. It was ... I don't know ... it was how we had kept her memory alive, and after that, it was like she was truly gone. Forever. The next year, when the holidays approached, I hoped ... perhaps he would return, and we would share those traditions once more, but he never did. I never saw him again. Sometimes I read news of him in London, but I did not know whether I would ever meet him again. I realized that second Christmas that I was truly alone in the world." She raised a hand to discreetly wipe at her damp lashes, then continued with heavy irony. "Well, except for *the baron*. Richard would not talk about my brother when he visited, but I had hoped when we became betrothed that ... perhaps I would see him when we went to London. If Richard had any intention of ever taking me to London."

"Annabel, I will take you to London. Once we are there, we will seek your brother out and make him explain!"

She looked at Philip, nonplussed. "There is no need. I do not expect you to manage my errant brother."

"There is every need. He is important to you, and I cannot let it stand that he abandoned you."

Annabel looked at him in wonder, her eyes filled with the same warm adoration she had displayed on their journey home from Baydon Hall. It filled Philip with both delight and trepidation. He was ill-equipped to handle young ladies and their emotions, as his disastrous first marriage had proved. He needed to maintain some distance between them so they could continue in the harmony of their bonds. However, he could not deny that he enjoyed her deep regard for him.

"Why would it matter to you?"

"Do you ever write to your brother? Do you have any communication with him?"

"None at all. Why do you ask?"

"I have some news to impart. There are rumors that Brendan may soon wed."

"What? How do you know that? Was it in the papers?"

"A scandal rag, actually. I rarely read them, but my man of business in London must have noted the mention of Ridley and sent it on to keep me informed about my relations."

"Confound it," she cursed, making Philip's lips quiver in amusement while he fought not to smile in the face of her unhappiness. His sweet wife was spirited, and he loved it, but this was not the appropriate time to display that.

"To be fair, my darling, I am not even sure if Brendan knows of your marriage to me yet, based on your lack of correspondence."

Her face cleared as she thought about what he said. "You are right. I did not inform him. Why would I think he would inform me?"

"Precisely. I think over the coming months, we should rectify the matter. I assume the baron has something to do with the estrangement."

"Either that or he just grew tired of his vexing sister."

"Delightfully vexing, my sweet, so I suspect the baron's hand in this." Annabel looked unconvinced. "Either way, Brendan's feelings do not factor. If my duchess wants her brother to pay her attention, then he will be required to comply. Besides, what man would turn up his nose at a connection with an all-powerful duke?"

Annabel's mouth curled into a smile. It gladdened Philip to see her recovering her good cheer. "I lo—appreciate you, husband. You make me feel … seen."

He smiled in response.

Annabel rose with a regretful sigh. "It is time for me to study."

She leaned over to pat his arm before walking away and Philip gathered his papers to read his mail, surprised to find a letter from Mrs. Thorne, since he had just visited her recently.

Reading through the missive containing unexpected news from the esteemed matron, he mentally calculated whether it was feasible to drive to Halmesbury and be back in time for his plans with Annabel.

∽

"Philip?"

"Yes, sweet?"

"I—how was your day?"

Annabel had hoped to tell him the truth about Richard, but as she rested in his comforting embrace, she could not bring herself to ruin the moment. She had thought of little else for the past two weeks. Earlier that day in the orangery, his concern for her connections had increased her guilt about hiding the truth. She also wrestled with another secret she was hesitant to confess: *I love you,* whispered her thoughts. *And you married me by mistake. Your cousin did not corrupt your late bride with his rakish ways.*

The warring emotions in her mind made peace elusive, save for the rare tranquility she found in Philip's arms.

"Excellent," he replied. "Mrs. Thorne is pleased with the progress at Halmesbury Home. The children are thriving under her guidance. She mentioned something important we should discuss over breakfast—too detailed for tonight."

"I love y—that you are such a good man."

He hugged her warmly, the strength of his embrace reassuring her. "And I love you are meeting with the tenants to discuss the school."

"Education is a passion of mine," she confessed. "I taught one of our young maids to read after giving her a copy of *Sense and Sensibility* for her birthday. I did not realize it would embarrass her. Mrs. Harris explained Caroline could not read, so I carved out time daily to teach her. It felt wonderful to make up for my mistake."

Philip smiled down at her. "I agree—reading is a gift everyone should experience. It opens the world."

Annabel hesitated, then asked, "Speaking of gifts, I was wondering...you know, that way you make me feel cherished and seen? How might I do the same for you?" Her cheeks flushed at her boldness, but her sincerity won out.

Philip chuckled, tucking a stray curl behind her ear. "You already do."

She laughed softly, the weight of her secrets momentarily lifting. Their shared warmth enveloped her like a cocoon, a space where love might take root, even amid so much left unsaid. Without making the decision, her lips formed the words she had had contained in her heart. "I love you, Philip, I love you so much!"

Philip stilled in shock as Annabel cringed in dismay

I love you? I love you so much?

She had been bottling up too many secrets, and one of them had come spilling out of her mouth.

CHAPTER SEVENTEEN

"Everywhere I see bliss, from which I alone am irrevocably excluded."

Mary Shelley's Frankenstein

∽

Philip froze as a turmoil of emotions hit him. On the one hand, he felt joy. Other than his parents, no one had ever said that to him. On the other hand, he was horrified. Why horror was not clear, other than *no one had ever told him that!*

He had wanted to win Jane's love but never had. Since her death, he had had no thoughts or hopes of love, just partnership.

Annabel squirmed before babbling out with high nerves, "I mean I love *that you care about my happiness*, I love *that* so much."

Philip rolled away and sat up. Uncertain what to say or

do, he jumped from the bed and walked to the washbasin. Pouring water from the jug, he dampened a towel and dabbed at his face, welcoming the chill as he attempted to gather his thoughts. Bemused, he returned to the bed.

Annabel flinched away from him and scrambled to the side of the bed and turned her back to him while she cleaned herself. "Do not concern yourself. My apologies. I did not mean to say that to you or put you under any pressure, so no need to concern yourself … I-I am sorry." She slowed down on the last, her voice thick. He perceived she was trying to not cry and felt appalled. What did one say next? It was all … so unexpected, and he did not know how he felt, so how could he respond?

"Annabel, I hold you in the highest esteem. You are attractive and vibrant and smart as a whip. I—"

"Please, Philip, it is all right. You do not have to say anything. This changes nothing. I am not expecting anything. Can we pretend I did not say it … please!" Her shoulders shook slightly as she lost the battle to hold back her tears. He could hear her muffled sniffs beneath her heaving breath.

His heart was breaking. He did not know what to do in this situation; he was so ill-equipped to handle such emotions. His first wife had despised him, and his new wife had surprised him with a declaration of love he was unprepared to hear. He floundered, staring at his miserable, sweet Annabel hunched in the far corner of the enormous bed. He sifted through his thoughts and tried again.

"Annabel, I admire you. You are courage and loyalty and honor. You fill my life—"

"*Richard did not betray you!*" she yelled at the wall she was facing.

"What?"

"Jane Marley was born a twin!" she blurted out. "His name was Richard. He died falling out of a tree when they were ten, and Jane was never the same again. She called for him for many months after he died, suffering from nightmares that she woke screaming from. Mary told me all about it when I questioned her after I read about the Marley family in Debrett's *Peerage*."

"What?" Philip felt like his mind was coming undone.

"I am not loyal or honorable. I'm definitely not brave. I did not tell you when I discovered the truth. I hoped you would never find out. So, you see, you do not owe me any declarations of love. I do not deserve them. I wanted to be selfish. I did not want to tell you that Richard might have hurt me, but he never betrayed you. You should find Richard. You deserve to have a friend. The one friend that did not betray you or keep any secrets, as it turns out."

Philip had not experienced such confusion since his late wife's illness and death. He could not think until one point flew out to hit him square on.

Richard did not betray me!

He had thrown his best friend out of his house and cut off all communication with him, *and Richard had done nothing to deserve it!* He had stolen the man's bride, justifying his desire for Annabel with the fact that Richard deserved it.

"Is this why we had that strange conversation about the Marley family?"

Annabel tensed. Philip waited during the pregnant pause until she finally answered, "Yes."

"Faith! I need to speak to Richard!"

"Yes."

"He should be in residence at Saunton Park at this time of the year. If I leave at first light, I can be there by the evening. I must take care of this, and then I will return. I ... emotions are turbulent at this moment, and ... I think ... I think it would be best for us both to spend a day or two clearing our heads, and we can talk when I return. Does that make sense?"

"Yes."

Philip barely noticed Annabel's dull response as he hurried to dress, his mind distracted by the implications of how he had severed a close relationship over a ridiculous misunderstanding. He needed to clear this matter up—*stuff!* He had just stolen the man's bride without the slightest twinge of conscience!

The man may have done ill to Annabel, but not himself, and although the outcome would not have differed, the execution could have been more adroit had he known there was no reason to be personally outraged with the man.

∽

As Philip rushed from her room, Annabel stared vacantly at the wall in front of her. She could not believe what a muck she had made of her promising new marriage. She found she did not like herself as she thought about how she had suppressed her discovery.

And justified it.

Philip had deserved to know about Richard. She should have taken her chances and told him straightaway, put his happiness first. Instead, she had been selfish and hidden the truth. She had broken trust with her husband.

Maybe they could have overcome the discovery, but her

subsequent silence had assuredly ruined any hope of trust between them. Annabel dropped her head into her hands as wrenching sobs escaped, tearing through her chest. She knew not if her tears were for Philip's dismay when she had blurted out her feelings, or remorse for her own despicable betrayal. She knew only that her heart was cracking as she pressed a hand down on it to ease the agony.

Annabel thought about the irony that Richard had remained true to his friendship with Philip, but had brought them together through their misunderstanding. Apparently, the earl possessed loyalty. Perhaps there was just something too unlovable about Annabel to earn any of that loyalty for herself. She simply had not been important enough for Richard to remain true to her. Surely her recent actions in withholding the truth from Philip, a truth that would have helped him regain his friendship, spoke to her unlovable nature. Perhaps she was more her awful father's daughter than her beloved mother's.

Things were falling apart, and her mother had never seemed so distant and long gone. For the first time, she no longer could imagine Mama's voice guiding her. She could not bear to think about what her mother would have to say about her recent behavior.

She sat alone in the empty room and thought about how Mama had passed away and left her. Brendan had abandoned her, Richard had betrayed her, and now her husband would surely desert her. It felt like history repeating itself yet again, but this time, there was no one to blame. Her dreams of romantic love with her husband tasted like ashes on her lips as she realized she had probably damaged any chance she had to earn his love.

She doubted she would have another opportunity now that she had proved her selfish nature. She massaged the ache in her chest, but there was no easing the pain of her breaking heart.

～

PHILIP RODE for an entire day in the wrong direction, thinking Richard was at his country seat in Saunton. When he reached Saunton Park, he learned Richard had left three days earlier for London. Philip stayed the night and then was forced to turn back to Avonmead to arrange for his carriage to drive him to London, which caused him to lose yet another day riding back. When he stopped at Avonmead, he had thought he should take a few minutes to ensure Annabel was well, but it was late at night and he concluded she was probably sleeping so would not appreciate him invading her room stinking of horse, sweat, and dust.

He stood at their connecting door, missing her, and concerned about the way they had left things. Raising his hand to turn the handle, he hesitated, then dropped it. He did not know what to say to her, as he had not yet sorted out his feelings, and if he could not return her love, he was going to have to work out how to let her down gently. He wished ... perhaps he wished he could just return in time to two nights earlier, when he had been with Annabel in her room, to address her outburst with more compassion. His poor wife had been so humiliated. He suspected he had not handled the outpouring about Jane and Richard Marley very well. He tried to recollect if he had actually responded to the revelations or had just run off to make amends with Saunton.

Philip attempted to recall their encounter, but his thoughts had been a whir after she told him she loved him, followed by the truth of Jane's defection turning out to be a false assumption.

Annabel is probably fast asleep, so this is not the time to talk.

Instead, he walked away from the door to wash up with cold water at his washstand before changing in a hurry and departing again with the ducal carriage for London.

He needed to find his cousin and make amends for betraying their friendship in such an awful manner. No wonder Richard had been so bitter the last time he had visited Avonmead, interrupting his dinner with Annabel. Philip had not the just cause he believed at the time to steal the man's bride.

He could only say the man's bride had begged him to intervene, and he could not bring himself to regret that aspect of the misunderstanding, but he regretted throwing Richard from his home when his friend had been trying to assist him with his first marriage. It was clear now why the earl had refused to enter Jane's rooms when they had argued in the hall;

Richard had known his presence could not be a comfort to her, as they had no connection to each other.

∼

ANNABEL LAY IN BED. She had heard Philip return, and he was moving around in the adjoining chambers. It was late, but she hoped he would enter her bedchamber to talk to her as he had on their wedding night. He had been gone for two days, and she had barely left her bed. She had been unwell —bilious and fatigued. Feeling guilty and disheartened had not helped. She lay huddled, listening to the sounds from the other room. She almost held her breath in anticipation when she heard him hesitate at their connecting door. But then his soft footfalls had moved away until she heard the far-off click of his door when he departed his chambers.

She thought about tossing the covers aside and racing to confront him, to demand that they talk, but the last thing her husband had said was that he needed to clear his head, and she still felt ashamed by her behavior, uncertain what she would say if she accosted him.

Perhaps her husband thought he had married the wrong woman and regretted their sudden nuptials. Would there be any more special moments in the future, the thrill of sweet kisses in the halls and shared rides on the estate? Or had he decided he had made a mistake in marrying her, and they would have an empty, loveless future ahead while she suffered from his disappointment in choosing the wrong wife?

Annabel knew she was spiraling, but she did not have the energy to fight it. She had elevated her hopes too high, and now she was paying the price for her overconfidence. She swallowed hard as a wave of nausea threatened.

She contemplated the events that had led her to Philip's study the day they had met, and she did not know whether to hate Richard or be grateful to him for setting her on this path. These had been the best weeks of her life, but at present she was disoriented about where things stood. She never knew such happiness was possible, but were the fates planning to snatch it away?

It was not fate; it was I. I betrayed Philip by concealing the truth for my own selfish purposes.

Annabel accepted the veracity of that statement.

She must recover her strength and go force her husband to have a conversation.

But not right now, she decided spiritlessly and turned to stare at the wall; the morning would be a better time. She would allow Philip to get some rest and then find him in the morning.

Except ... disappointment crept over her when she heard the distant sound of a carriage driving away from the mansion and she realized her husband had left again.

∼

LISTLESS AND TIRED, Annabel drifted in and out of restless sleep all night until midmorning. Prying her eyes open, her head pulsed in agonized exhaustion, her eyes feeling grainy and her lids too heavy to open more than a slit before she groaned and turned over to go back to sleep. She wondered if she had imagined the duke's almost-visit the night before, because her short bursts of sleep had been interspersed with dozens of disturbing dreams.

Had he really turned away from her door? Her thoughts drifted as if she were weightless in a gray fog. She could not focus long enough to recall the memory. Perhaps it had been a dream. Why would Philip return to Avonmead? All that waited for him here were memories of the first wife he had loved and lost, along with a new wife who had turned out to be devious.

Annabel did not like those thoughts, so she turned her mind back to memories. She drifted around moments with her mother and tried to avoid recent events. She could not think of Philip yet, not without an ache in the region of her heart.

She wondered vaguely whether it would be a good idea to rise and find something to do. Perhaps taking a walk would help.

Why, why did I tell him I loved him? Why did I hide the

truth about Richard Marley or trick Philip into that ridiculous discussion about Jane's family?

She vaguely recollected that she had thought about rising a few moments earlier to take a walk and start clearing her head. However, that would take energy and effort, and her body felt too boneless.

Later ... later she would get up and eat. Right now, she would sleep.

CHAPTER
EIGHTEEN

"Life, although it may only be an accumulation of anguish, is dear to me, and I will defend it."

Mary Shelley's Frankenstein

~

"Child, you have been in your room two days and the better part of another, and it is time to get up!" Mrs. Harris's roughened voice startled Annabel out of a doze.

"Mrs. Harris?" Annabel cracked an eye open to stare up at the perforated cornice of her magnificent mahogany bed, ivory and red drapes woven through to fall in majestic folds that she had kept drawn closed since taking to her chambers. The bed she had shared with the duke almost every night since their wedding. *But not since he had left her.*

"Yes, my girl, I'm here to ensure you eat a full breakfast and rise."

"Where is Mary?"

"Your lady's maid is worried about you and does not think she can talk sense into that thick head of yours, so she came to find me."

Annabel slowly turned onto her back and tilted her head to look at the housekeeper. "What makes you think you can?"

"Girl, if I must, I am going to drag you out of that bed and spoon-feed you until you eat an entire meal. I am quite aware that you have been picking at your meals and only had a minimum to eat. I will not stand for it. Sit up and start eating!"

Annabel knew there was no point in arguing. The cheerful older woman could turn quite stern and shrewish when she was determined to put her mothering hat on. Since Mama had died, Mrs. Harris was not afraid to get parental with her.

She struggled into a sitting position and beckoned for the tray. The smell of eggs and ham hit her, causing her stomach to heave in protest. She knew from experience that beginning with a small piece of fruit would open her appetite up, so she picked up an apple quarter and took a small bite. As she chewed, she realized she was relieved Mrs. Harris was here. Like Philip had fallen into a grieving period not so long ago, now she appeared to have done the same.

Sometimes, she mused, you just need someone to intercede when life gets too overwhelming. Someone like Mrs. Harris, who refused to allow a disastrous situation to fester in her vicinity. Mama would have been happy to know Annabel had such a loyal friend.

"My girl, I am going to have a bath prepared. You need to clean up and leave your bedchamber. There is more than one person to think of now, so it won't do to dawdle."

Annabel nodded and kept chewing on the apple. Swallowing was difficult with her throat locked up. Once she was done with the apple, she gingerly started on the eggs, sipping hot tea between mouthfuls. *Two of us to take care of?* How did her eating help Philip? He was not even in residence.

Annabel shrugged to herself and kept eating. As she ate, she felt her muscles relaxing and eating became easier. She acknowledged that barely eating the past couple days had been a poor choice, for the despair and nausea were now abating to a manageable level. Slowly she became more aware of the room around her—the sound of the servants filling the tub, birds chattering outside the window, the apparent gray pall that had lain over the bedchamber receding to reveal the true warm ivory, rich mahogany, and lush red.

She paused in her eating, feeling full. Mrs. Harris noticed and walked back over to the bed to peer at her tray. "Your Grace, you will need to eat more than that," she commanded in a menacing murmur, mindful of the other servants in the room.

"But—"

"Eat!" the housekeeper hissed.

Annabel gave a small nod and finished the eggs before picking at the ham.

She saw the housekeeper shooing the other servants out, the bath now ready. Annabel rushed to devour the ham before the housekeeper could scold her again.

Mrs. Harris walked back over and looked at the empty plates. She gave a nod. "That will do. Now finish that tea and come bathe."

Over the next thirty minutes, Mrs. Harris bullied her along to wash up, even washing her hair for her like she had when she was young. She had forgotten that many years ago, Mrs. Harris had started as her nanny. Mama and Mrs. Harris had bonded, becoming quite close, and Lady Filminster had promoted the older woman first to upper servant, then to housekeeper when the last one had retired.

"Mrs. Harris, how long were you with Mama?"

Mrs. Harris had been briskly massaging Annabel's scalp. She hesitated at the question before commencing with the washing, her voice suspiciously gruff as she spoke next. "I knew Catherine Ridley when she was a girl in torn dresses, chasing around after John Ridley like a shadow. She was a rapscallion, your mum."

"*John Ridley?*"

"Yes, child, your mama was betrothed to the baron's older brother. He cut a dashing figure, but he was wildly irresponsible, racing that thoroughbred the way he did. He died just weeks before they were to take their vows. I will never forgive that scoundrel for leaving her ladyship all alone."

"I did not know you had been with our family that long." Annabel fell silent. "I suppose that is how she came to be married to Father."

Mrs. Harris's fingers in her hair hesitated once more, but the old lady remained silent. As she poured warm water over Annabel's hair a few moments later, she spoke up. "I came to work in your mother's household just after my husband passed. Your mama was a steadfast girl. I never encountered a more courageous, loyal person. When she heard of my loss, she started bringing me gifts. Apples she had picked in the orchards. Flowers from the field—" The older woman's voice broke. She quickly recovered her composure to continue. "I loved your mama so much. You remind me of her."

"Thank you," Annabel croaked out past the lump in her throat.

"I was there for both times she was with child. First with Brendan and then you. She was so happy when you were born. *'Annabel will have the best of everything. She will be smart and live a long and happy life married to someone wonderful, Mrs. Harris!'* she used to tell me. She very much wanted to ensure you married for love."

Annabel brushed a tear with the back of her hand. "That is not to be, I am afraid. I mean ... the duke is wonderful, but he is not happy with me. I failed him. And then I scared him off."

"I do not presume to know His Grace well enough to remark on all that, but regardless, you have more than one person to think of now. And more than one way to experience love."

Annabel looked up into the housekeeper's round face to find her twinkling, hazel eyes. "I just said the duke—I don't think he is going to be around Avonmead anymore. At least ... I hope he will allow me to remain here at Avonmead and not send me to one of his other estates."

"Aye, but no matter where you are, there will soon be two of you. And you will need to provide lots of love when that happens, so there will be no time for moping from here on out."

Annabel's face scrunched as she tried to make sense of the older woman's cryptic remarks. "There are already two of us, and one of us is not here. The duke is in London, and I am unsure that he will return."

"If the duke did return, that would make three."

Annabel wondered if the older woman was having an apoplexy of some sort. The housekeeper returned her gaze steadily. Annabel stared back at her without comprehension until she finally spoke. "Girl, how long have you lived at Avonmead?"

"About four or so weeks."

"Uh huh," the other woman agreed. "And how long would you say it has been since you had your monthly courses?"

Annabel shook her head. "Not since before I came to Avo—*NO*!"

"Yes."

"No!"

"Girl, you have been fatigued this week, no?" Annabel nodded.

"And your bosom seems a little fuller than I recall." Annabel nodded again.

"And Mary says she has to ensure your chamberpot is sorted every couple of hours since you took to your chambers. Bladder pressing on you, is it?"

"Oh."

"And, to the best of my recollection, you were never really fond of oranges, but before you took to your bed, I seem to recall you visiting the orangery daily for at least a couple of weeks and seeing orange rinds coming back to the kitchen on your trays."

Annabel's head whirled with the implications. "I am with child?"

"Yes, now get up. I want to dress you so the doctor can come up and examine you."

"The doctor?"

"I took the liberty of sending for him. You can dock my wages for being a saucy, overbearing servant if you like. But you will see the doctor in a few moments. It is rude to keep him waiting."

Annabel's eyes filled with tears as she rose to her feet.

Her heart filled with gratitude as she draped her wet arms around the older woman, drenching the housekeeper's gray serge with bathwater. "Thank you, Mrs. Harris."

As she took the towel offered by her lifelong friend, Annabel realized she had much to live for—the same wonderful friend who had always been with her, and now a babe of her own. Perhaps she might even reconcile with Philip. However, the future could be good with or without him. Although she couldn't help hoping that it would be with him, somehow, if he could find it in his heart to forgive her.

∾

PHILIP LISTENED to the clack of the carriage wheels hitting against the roadway. The trip to London seemed interminable, and he had far too much time alone with his thoughts. He thought of Annabel's assertions of love. It was deuced uncomfortable. He was uncertain how to proceed. Love was not a good idea, if it, in fact, existed. Once upon a time, he had believed himself in love with Jane. It felt like a lifetime ago, but it had not taken long to realize that his feelings for his first wife had been infatuation. They had never shared a genuine connection. How could love exist in the absence of communication and trust? The two of them had been strangers in every way that mattered, and this new information from Annabel only reinforced that fact.

Now Annabel believed she was in love with him, but that, too, was infatuation. They had shared blissful weeks together, so it was natural that a young woman would fancy herself in love. But love, did love truly exist? Only for a privileged few, such as his parents, who had shared deep bonds of friendship and admiration. Besides his parents, had he ever seen a true love match? A true partnership of minds, synchronous hearts and souls with a deep passion for each other? Nay, Annabel was misguided about their amicable companionship. They were just friends ... who happened to enjoy time alone together.

He had the utmost regard for his gorgeous wife, but he would need to create some distance between them so that she could realize on her own that her feelings of love were just inflated by their companionship. Perhaps he would reduce the time he spent with her. They could spend the day apart as they had done in the afternoons. He would still spend the evenings with her because he ... because he ... because he had a responsibility to sire an heir.

Philip felt much better once he had determined that their nights of marital relations could continue—he was just taking care of his familial obligations. During the day ... during the day, he would keep his distance so she could work out her feelings in a manner which would let her down easily about forming deep emotional attachments. He would spare her the pain of rejection or embarrassment while maintaining their companionship. She was a smart girl, and she would figure it out.

His mind settled, Philip relaxed back into the gray squabs. Everything would work out well ... without the muddle of emotions.

CHAPTER NINETEEN

"I was cursed by some devil, and carried about with me my eternal hell."

Mary Shelley's Frankenstein

Night was falling when the carriage reached Mayfair. Street lamps cast a glow onto the steps of Richard's townhouse as Philip ran up to pound on the door. When no one responded, he pounded again. Eventually, a young footman in full livery, flushed from running, opened the carved door to greet him.

"I am looking for Saunton," Philip demanded.

The footman's eyes widened in surprise. "His lordship is in Saunton. We are not expecting him for at least two weeks."

Philip scowled and cursed, causing the young man to wince ever so slightly while he fought to maintain his aplomb. Philip did not care if the footman reacted to his outburst as he bounded back down the stone steps to settle back into his waiting carriage.

"White's!" he bellowed at the coachman as he closed the door behind him. Richard had not come to his home, so he must be living at one of his clubs, carousing the evenings away. Philip would walk into every club in London to find him if needed. This matter must be settled straightaway.

An hour later, Philip strode down the steps away from the bow window of White's. Traffic on the roads had held them up far longer than his patience could handle, and when he searched through the club, no one there had seen Richard in at least a month. The earl had to be hiding out from his usual cronies.

Philip stood by his carriage under the street lamp, thinking. Where should he try next?

"Alfred Club," he commanded before pushing his way back into the dark interior of his carriage. Alfred Club was dry for Richard's tastes, but he liked to go there to debate with men of letters. One had to debate without the aid of liquor, but it made for an evening of creative thinking.

As the carriage turned off Piccadilly onto Albemarle Street, Philip looked out the window and noted they were driving past the publishing offices of John Murray. It brought to mind Annabel's love of *Pride and Prejudice*, and he pondered the possibility of locating a first edition for his wife as the carriage drew up outside Alfred Club. He had missed Annabel over the past few days of hard travel, and he wanted to return to her as soon as possible. A gift would not be amiss, considering he needed to ease her feelings of infatuation and ... and he enjoyed her happiness.

Alfred Club turned out to be uneventful. The club had been full to the rafters with members, but no one had seen Richard in some time. An author of several popular books had scratched his head and offered—of no help whatsoever—"I thought Lord Saunton was getting married. Is he not in the country with his bride?"

Philip had turned and left in disgust. Where was his rascal of a cousin? This search had taken up days.

As he stepped back into the night, he was thankful for the nighttime entertainments of London, which allowed him to keep searching unhampered. The last thing he needed was to head to his own townhouse in a futile attempt to sleep. Annabel was waiting for him at home in Avonmead, and he was afraid he had terribly botched that last conversation they had had several nights ago. He did not need a restless night turning the details over in his mind.

As he approached his carriage once more, he racked his brain for another location to look for Richard. He could not recall whether Richard kept a membership at Arthur's Club. He should have planned out a route to the clubs systematically instead of bouncing around London in this haphazard manner.

Oh well, too late to be concerned with that. "Arthur's Club on St. James's Street," he called up to the coachman, who gave a brisk nod in response.

The carriage continued down Albemarle Street and traversed around the block before reentering, facing the opposite direction. Soon Albemarle turned into St. James's Street as the carriage drove slowly through the evening traffic of carriages and horses of gentlemen visiting their clubs, and they drew to a stop in front of Arthur's Club.

Sometime later, Philip was standing back in the street. Arthur's Club was as lavish as he recalled from his last visit, predating his first marriage, and he had encountered many old acquaintances who wanted to talk to him, causing his search to drag out endlessly until he had escaped after determining that Richard "was in the country getting married, don't you know, old chap?" As a matter of fact, he did *not* know.

A thought occurred to him while he stood out on the lamplit street. Did Richard not have many genuine friends? Was the earl like him, surrounded by hordes of people but always alone? Philip reflected on the years since their separation. He had to admit that losing his friendship with Saunton had left a hole in his life, Richard being one of the few genuine friendships he maintained. It had not helped him cope with the loss of his wife when he had thrown out his friend right when he needed him most. If only he had not so quickly jumped to conclusions.

On the other hand, if events had not unfolded in that precise manner, he would not now have his delightful Annabel waiting for him at Avonmead. She would be married to Richard now, not him. The past had already taken place. What remained was to mend this misunderstanding with Richard before taking full advantage of his new life with Annabel, because … because … because they had a future generation of Markhams to produce, he told himself.

∼

THE LIBRARY WAS in shadows as heavy rain drummed outside the wall of windows. Annabel looked around her at the piles of amassed books, not quite interested but nevertheless determined to keep herself busy because she missed Philip and their shared routines. It had been six days since she had last spoken to him. She was back in action, taking walks and forcing herself to eat full meals. And she had read her new Debrett's volumes cover to cover, taking copious notes. The effort might be wasted if Philip planned to keep his distance and not take her to London with him, but she did not have much to do while she awaited the duke's return.

She had intended to visit the nursery to make plans, but she felt uncertain about her future. Her husband loved Avonmead, but it seemed certain that he did not return her love. How angry was he at her error in judgment? He had already concluded in the few minutes they had argued that Annabel had known about Richard Marley for a while, having flung that question about her clumsy interrogation regarding the Marley family.

She sighed heavily. When had she become so stupid? *You fall in love one time and suddenly you want to do anything and everything you can to earn the admiration of your heart's desire.*

If only she had told him, she would not have felt guilt-ridden with secrets and perhaps the second error of blurting out her heart would have never occurred either.

Earning his love had been a futile endeavor from the start. His heart belonged to the exquisite Jane, who had rejected him and closed off his heart. The young woman who had made the duke fall in love in the ballrooms of high society, just as Annabel had first envisioned when she had gazed upon her likeness. Jane, who had captured him with her beautiful features, soft blonde curls, blue eyes, and rosebud lips. Not to mention her accomplishments with the pianoforte, needlework and, she surmised, watercolor paints. The perfect debutante and exact opposite of Annabel in every way. All Annabel could hope for was to earn his affections.

I promise to not have unreasonable expectations.

She would love their baby, and she would earn Philip's friendship again, if he would allow it. And she would keep her admiration to herself, shut inside her heart where it belonged! She decided her husband would feel compelled to sort out their disagreement, if for no other reason than he was a gentleman who believed in fidelity.

Her advice to Philip had been correct. One could drive oneself insane with these thoughts bouncing around one's skull. She sat up and rubbed her belly, smiling wanly as she recalled stating that very idea to Philip less than a month ago. If these thoughts kept chasing around her head, she would be forced to talk to herself out loud, just to get them out of her head and out in the open where she could hear them. Judge the logic of them. If that happened, she wouldn't have to worry about being sent to another estate. She would be sent to Bedlam instead.

~

IT HAD TAKEN Philip the better part of one evening plus another day to inquire at all the clubs and gaming hells he could recall Saunton mentioning. He had been forced to go to Markham House, his London townhouse, in the early hours to allow his footman, his coachman, and himself to eat and rest. With a fresh change of horses, they had recommenced their crisscross of London's districts.

When he finally succeeded in locating the earl, it was at the Stratford Club on Little Portland Street in Mayfair. They must have sailed past the club multiple times in their search while Richard had played whist through the night.

Philip did not have a membership, but when he made himself known, and whom he sought, they ushered him in.

He had expected to find Richard deep in his cups or

buried in a high-stakes card game. In his mind, Richard would be as drunk as ... well, drunk as a lord. He was taken aback to find Richard seated in the shadows at a back table—alone—facing the room, and sober, in a frightening way, his face severe as he surveyed the men playing cards throughout the room. His affable cousin did not look ... affable.

Richard ignored Philip's approach until the duke stood right next to him, where he hesitated, unsure what to say.

"I hope you are here to apologize for stealing Annabel," Richard stated after a long pause, tilting his head back to focus on Philip's towering form standing above him. "I am still quite angry about that."

Philip took the seat beside him and opened his mouth to apologize. Then he shut it, realizing the one thing he could never apologize for was taking Annabel away from him. He wondered at this, why he felt that way, before attempting another reply. He did not know what words he would say until he heard himself speak. "Annabel deserved better. You did not treat her well."

"You are better?"

Philip took a deep breath. He had not expected his meeting to be easy, but it surprised him just how difficult it was to sit here, to talk to his estranged cousin, his—how maudlin a sentiment—former best friend. "Saunton, Annabel has uncovered the truth. That you never betrayed me with Jane. I am here to apologize for misjudging your intentions during that visit three years ago."

Saunton's lids slitted into a suspicious glare. "What do you mean, Annabel uncovered the truth? What truth?"

"Jane had a twin brother."

This was met with an expression of perplexity. "And?"

"His name was Richard Marley."

Saunton's face gradually cleared as he digested the information. "I see. And Annabel believes that Richard Marley is the one Jane was calling for in her fever?"

"Marley died when she was young, and apparently, the loss was ... traumatic."

"Ah." Richard looked down at his untouched drink. Philip waited for his cousin to sort through his private thoughts. Eventually Saunton looked up, not quite meeting his eye, but staring somewhere beyond Philip's shoulder. "I have missed you," he said in a hoarse whisper. "Her Grace was a beautiful woman, but I swear I would never have interfered between you and your late wife. I tried to tell you at the time. I could never have done such a thing to you. Especially when I was present because you had requested my help."

"I know that now. And, for jumping to conclusions and failing to hear you out, I offer my profound apologies." Philip cleared his throat, chagrined by the force of his relief at reuniting with his cousin. He was grateful to Annabel for clearing up their misunderstanding, despite her personal history with the earl providing her with good reason to not reveal the truth. He had an inkling she had finally disclosed it for his sake, because she wanted him to be happy.

Saunton coughed into his hand, looking abashed at revealing his sentiments. "I have had a deuced awful month since encountering you at Baydon Hall. Quite depressed, in fact, old chap. Have not even had the will to drink or visit any beds. Can you imagine? It is hell, I tell you!"

Philip snorted in response. "I missed you. I did not know how much I missed you until I married Annabel and rediscovered the joys of friendship."

They both sat in silence, staring at the table between them, lost in their own thoughts.

Finally, Saunton looked up. "The joys of friendship? Is that what you and Annabel share? How is that different from what I was offering her, then?"

Philip chuckled as he thought of his wife. "Annabel is amazing. She is funny and kind. She loves looking after people. She loves looking after me ..." Philip grinned as he thought of their past weeks together, his chest warming in fondness. "She is clever and adventurous. I can talk to her about anything, and she jolts me from my maudlin thoughts. I could spend a hundred years with her and never grow tired of her company. I think about her all the time, and I missed her more this week than I missed you in the past three years."

Saunton tilted his head in a bemused query. "Halmesbury, what you just described, that is not friendship, I do not think." His cousin was staring at him with a strange expression when Philip refocused on him, bringing his mind back to the present. Philip frowned in confusion.

His cousin continued. "Do not misunderstand me. Annabel is all of those things. That is why I believed she was the one woman I could abide marrying. Losing my chance with her has made me feel at odds for the past month. I do not know if I want to drink myself under a table, sober up, change my life completely, or just return to what I was doing before the idea of marriage entered my head. But what you just described, and the way your face lit up while you were talking ... I do not think you were describing friendship, cousin."

Philip stared at Saunton for some time, trying to make sense of what the man was implying. Slowly, he collected his wits. "What are you saying? You think I love her? Why do you think ... that ... that ... Oh ... blast ... I do ... I love her ... I loved her the moment she stole into my study and asked me to come to her aid! How could I not? She was the very antithesis of Jane, all boldness and brightness driving back the shadows I had been living in. She always says what she thinks, and she makes me talk when I am troubled. Jane would not even be in the same room with me, let alone talk to me, but my Annabel seeks me out to smother me with warm affection—"

Richard smirked. "Must be nice to be wanted."

"And I ran off nearly a week ago to hunt you down! Right after she told me she loved me, I ran off! What must she think?"

"She probably thinks you are a terrible blackguard who does not love her. You failed to mention any reciprocation within that little narrative?"

"Hell, Annabel is right! If you do not say these things out loud to someone, these thoughts get trapped in your head until they turn into deranged, illogical conclusions. I was so startled that this remarkable, vivacious woman could love me, I left her crying in her bedchamber. Botheration! She was pleading for me to forget that she voiced her feelings and apologizing for uncovering the truth about Jane's brother!" Philip's chair tipped as he jumped up, but he reached out and grabbed it before it fell over. "I have to go ... I have to go tell my wife I love her."

Saunton raised his tumbler in toast. "Long live true love."

Philip gave a short bow. "Once again, my friend, my sincere apologies for doubting you. I will make some time for you so we can reconnect once I have sorted out this matter with Annabel. But do not come to Avonmead. You still acted like an utter dog with Annabel, and I don't want to force your company on her unless she wishes to see you."

The earl grimaced. "Understood. Do not come to Avonmead unless I am invited. I won't say I don't still resent you stealing my bride, but now that you have her, go make it right, Halmesbury. She is rather special, you know."

Philip assented and turned to walk back out of the club.

"Oh, Halmesbury?" Philip stopped.

"Thank you ... for coming to find me. I find myself ... feeling ... uplifted somehow. I think I needed this ... our reconciliation."

Philip's lips curved. "Me, too, cousin. Me, too."

CHAPTER
TWENTY

"The mountains and the waters had become my sole acquaintance."

Mary Shelley's Frankenstein

∽

Philip returned to Markham House after his conversation with Richard. He was desperate to return to Avonmead, but he had not slept or eaten properly in days. It would not do to drop dead from exhaustion on the long journey. As he attempted to sleep alone in his massive state bed, he tossed. Then turned. Then tossed some more.

He had the awful feeling that he had mishandled these past few days. Was Richard right? Did Annabel consider him to be an unmitigated cad after their last discourse? He attempted once more to think of what he had said in response to her declaration. He recollected her words with extraordinary accuracy, but could not bring his own responses to mind. Had he not said *anything*? Is that why he could not recall his own words?

If he had said *nothing* in response, what must Annabel think? Did she believe he was angry with her? How could he be angry? She had reconciled him with his cousin after he had made erroneous assumptions for years. Did she now think her love was unwanted? He had never been the recipient of such regard, apart from his parents who were long since departed from this world. He was not quite sure what to do when admired so wholly. It made him both uncomfortable and grateful.

It would be as much as two more days before he would see her again. He wished he had not left her alone in her despair.

"I love you care about my happiness! I love that so much." He recalled the anguish in her voice as she had attempted to retract her declaration. That was before she realized it was futile. The words could not be unsaid. Then she had shifted to apologizing for affections. *"—please, Philip, it is all right. You do not have to say anything. This changes nothing. I'm not expecting anything. Can we pretend I did not say it ... please!"*

His chest tightened at the memory, and he wanted to kick himself for the foolish platitudes he had uttered instead of taking her in his arms and telling her his heart. He needed to get back to Avonmead. He cringed as he recollected his idiotic conclusions in his carriage on the way to London. No true pairing of the minds? No honest moments between them? He had never experienced such closeness, nor shared so many of his private thoughts with any living soul. He had convinced himself that what Annabel felt was infatuation, when they had truly forged a deep and personal connection. It was ridiculous. *He* was ridiculous. He had been so afraid of love that he had rejected his glorious Annabel, causing her to *apologize* for her affection.

His immaturity was mortifying, his handling of the first genuine connection he had ever experienced with a woman was an embarrassment. Philip turned over again, but there was no comfort to be found in his heavenly, luxurious bed while the discomfort torturing him lay within his conscience, and he had no means of pacifying it.

After a fruitless night of sleep, or lack of it, Philip had opened his eyes from an unsatisfying doze to find light streaming between his curtains. He jumped out of bed, eager to dress and eat before leaving London. As he called for a footman to valet for him, he came to a standstill. It was premature to leave London. There was something he needed to do first. Reaching his wife would have to wait a little longer.

~

ONCE AGAIN, he searched London for yet another member of the peerage. He could have sent a footman out to do the reconnaissance, but Philip feared going mad if he did not occupy his mind, so he conducted the search himself. First, he sought out Richard at Stratford Club to ascertain the location of the gentleman he sought.

The earl had surprisingly been up before midday, eating breakfast, and had been a fount of information regarding probable locations. Saunton, however, had declined to discuss anything he might know about personal matters. Nevertheless, Philip now had a list of places to survey. On this occasion, to save valuable hours, he had planned his search in an ordered manner. His theory was that he would see Annabel sooner if he approached this new hunt with efficiency.

He had begun his search at the Ridley townhouse just off Grosvenor Square. It had not taken long to reach the stucco building. He looked up at the four-story façade and drew a deep, calming breath. He hoped his search would be over immediately as he mounted the stone steps. Reaching the door, he eyed the brass knocker formed in the shape of a lion's head. Resolutely, he lifted his hand to grasp the ring and bring it down with a heavy, methodical thumping. And then he waited for signs of life from within.

When a butler appeared, resplendent in his black suit and pompous attitude, Philip handed him a card. The stoic butler bowed and asked him to wait in the hall. The duke had trouble standing still as impatience sung through his limbs. He needed to handle this matter and leave the city for home. His true home, where his very heart waited for him.

At least, based on the butler taking his card, it appeared his hunt was over, he reassured himself.

The middle-aged butler of average height had heavy footsteps, Philip discovered when the man returned a few moments later.

"Mr. Ridley is not receiving guests," he intoned.

"Hmm. Were you aware that Miss Annabel Ridley is now the Duchess of Halmesbury?"

The servant's nostrils flared ever so slightly. "Indeed? I was not aware."

"Yes, indeed. That means that the Baron of Filminster is now my beloved father-in-law."

There was a brief flicker of anxiety in the older man's eyes as Philip stared him down.

"I would hate to report back to the baron, who, if I am

not mistaken, is the true master of this household, that I was shown the door when I came to visit."

The butler looked undecided for a fraction of a second. "Please follow me, Your Grace."

As the manservant led him down the hall past the main stairs, Philip noted that the townhouse's furnishings were old-fashioned. The wallpaper was faded, and the carpets worn. From what he knew of the baron, wealth was not an issue, so he assumed the neglect of the home was because of the baron's isolation in Filminster. Why would he update a residence he never intended to visit, after all?

Moments later, the butler opened a door. Philip stepped into what appeared to be the study, while the butler quickly made a hasty retreat.

A gentleman about twenty-five years of age with a full mane of chestnut curls looked up from the desk where he was writing.

"Who are you?" demanded the younger man, his brandy eyes narrowed in surprise.

"Mr. Ridley?"

"I said, who are you? And what are you doing in my study?"

"I believe this is the study of Lord Filminster, if I am not mistaken."

"What is this?" growled the man as he pushed his seat back and rose to glower at Philip.

"I have come from Halmesbury to seek your help, Mr. Ridley."

"I do not know anyone from Halmesbury, so you have the wrong man. I demand you leave this instant. Why did Michaels show you in here?"

"I am the Duke of Halmesbury. I am married to your sister, Annabel."

The man flinched before flopping back down into his chair.

"Annabel is not my sister."

"You are Mr. Brendan Ridley?"

The baron's heir gave a curt nod. He bore a remarkable resemblance to Annabel, causing Philip to feel quite nostalgic. "Then you are Annabel's brother. My brother-in-law, in fact."

"Annabel is not my sister."

"So you have said. Do you care to explain?"

"Not to some stranger who has intruded my home."

Philip shuttered his expression as he squashed his irritation. First, the man had abandoned his sister to their horrible father, and now he was being an obnoxious dolt. Philip reminded himself he could either get angry or be effective. He was here for Annabel, so … so he smiled politely and continued. "I see. That is fair. I think we should start again. I am pleased to meet you, Mr. Brendan Ridley. I am Philip Markham, the Duke of Halmesbury."

Philip gave a polite, formal bow. "We need not stand on convention, as quite recently we became related. Call me Halmesbury … or Philip, if you like. I am married to your sister, the fair Annabel, who has missed you these past years, and I am here on her behalf. May I sit?" He gestured at the chairs placed in front of the desk.

The other man sighed in resignation and waved his hand to the seats.

Philip strode forward. Flicking his coattails, he sat.

"Please explain what you meant when you said that Annabel is not your sister."

The man looked away, reluctance obvious in his demeanor.

"Mr. Ridley, we are related to each other. I am the soul

of discretion, and I care about the members of my new family. I seek to understand what has led to the estrangement between you and your sister. Anything we discuss here is private, and you appear to be a man who may find it favorable to unburden yourself?"

The man swallowed, the only sign he was listening while he stared toward the hearth, the dancing flames reflected in his eyes.

"Mr. Ridley, I believe your mother was a kind and caring woman who would be most disappointed to find her children scattered and bereft. Please, tell me your story. Is the baron involved in the dissolution of your family?"

The man tensed. Philip could sense the younger peer would talk if he waited and, as he had provided him with several good reasons to do so, all that remained was patient silence. Settling back into his chair, he checked himself from saying anything further.

Several moments passed. The silence was so thick that Philip imagined he could hear his own heart pounding.

"I thought Annabel was to marry Richard Balfour?"

"There was an unfortunate incident with the earl and a young maid who worked in your fath—" Philip caught himself. If Annabel did not think of the baron with any sentiment, the likelihood was that his heir would not either. "—the baron's kitchens," he finished.

The other man groaned and sank his face into his hands. "Saunton betrayed her?"

Philip gave a quick nod.

"And Annabel knows that?"

"Your sister found them."

Mr. Ridley kept his face buried in his hands as he gave a moan of distress and shook his head in denial. Philip's compassion ignited when he realized the brother did, in fact, care about Annabel, even though he had not visited or corresponded with her these past four years. After a few moments, the other man dropped his hands as he looked up to confront Philip.

"I was so afraid of that when he told me of their betrothal. But because of their long-standing relationship, I had hoped my doubts were unfounded. How are you involved? How ... do you come to be married to Annabel?"

"She sought me out as a last resort when the baron insisted that the wedding would proceed. I happened to need a wife and Annabel was—is delightful, so ... so I ..." Philip shrugged. "... rescued her from her situation, I guess you could say."

Ridley shook his head. "The old devil would have forced her to proceed?" It was a rhetorical question, so Philip did not answer. Pausing for a while, his reluctant host finally continued. "I have heard of you. You are a widower who does charitable works. I believe I read an article in *The Gentleman's Magazine* a couple of months back. You ... care for Annabel?"

"Indeed, Mr. Ridley. I esteem her with every fiber of my being. She is extraordinary."

"Yes," the man did not hesitate in agreeing, "she is."

They both sat in contemplative silence while Brendan Ridley appeared to take his measure before finally speaking again. "What I say, you will maintain in privacy?"

"On pain of death."

Ridley drew a deep breath. "For Annabel, I will share with you, but I will kill you with my bare hands if I hear any word of this getting out."

Philip inclined his head in acceptance of Ridley's terms. "On pain of death."

ANNABEL WAS ENJOYING a visit with the wife of one of their tenant farmers, Mrs. James, who was swollen with child. It could not be more than a matter of days before Mrs. James would usher her babe into the world. It was unexpectedly pleasant to be sitting with the mother of two as Annabel grew accustomed to the idea that her own body would be changing.

Mrs. James was a lively woman in her late twenties with a mass of untamed brown curls attempting to escape her hairpins. She had red cheeks and tanned skin, and her brown eyes sparkled with life as she enjoyed the preserves that Annabel had brought along in a basket of gifts for the family. The little James girl, Hannah, a perfect miniature version of her mother, was shelling peas in a bowl with her tiny hands while her mother watched on like a hawk. The vigilant parent jumped up to join her child at the other side of the crude kitchen table when she noticed something was wrong. Gently, the woman showed her daughter how to shell without squashing the plump orbs. While the two chattered, Annabel took a moment to be nostalgic about her possible future.

As the days lingered with relentless vigor, it felt like the time since Philip had left her behind at Avonmead was infinite. Each second that passed felt like a minute. Every minute an hour. Every hour a day. By the time she laid her head on her pillow each night, it was as if a week had passed since the night before. Annabel's thoughts had swung every which way as she tried to anticipate what the future would bring. In the past day, she had become convinced that he might abandon her in the country as Richard had planned to do—which she hoped was just a ridiculous notion prompted by the fact that she did not know what was happening with the duke. Talking with the stable master, she had learned that Philip had left for London, which at least explained the midnight departure several days earlier.

Soon it would be Brendan's birthday, which marked the time they would have begun their holiday traditions and a particularly sad time of the year for her. She had not seen her brother in four years, and it gave her precedent for concern. Could she expect her husband of a few weeks to return to her, or would he abandon her to rusticate, as Brendan had done?

As a wife, she did not legally exist to make her own decisions, and he would decide her fate when he eventually decided to return. She had a babe on the way, but if the duke sent her away to another one of his estates to put distance between them, would he keep the little one here? Did she need to keep her heart disengaged even from her own child, lest it be broken in a few months when she might be forced to part with him or her?

It was bittersweet to watch the happy familial interplay while her own future was uncertain. She acknowledged to herself that she was angry with the duke, who had promised her they would talk. Loneliness was a constant companion, and she wished once more that her own mama was still here to talk to.

She deserved to know what her husband planned to do about the recent revelations. Had he found Richard? Had they sorted out their disagreement? Did the fact that there was no cause for his anger at Richard affect their marriage? Had it been a significant factor in his decision to marry her?

She had the right to know where things stood. Annabel

beat back her resentment of her missing husband and steeled her nerves.

Pushing her conflicting thoughts to the back of her mind, she breathed in the fragrant tea and took another sip while she waited for Mrs. James to return to her seat. She would visit every tenant farmhouse on their lands, meet every Avonmead wife and mother, before she shed another tear.

Mrs. James returned to her seat and picked up her discarded teacup, raising it to her lips to sip before continuing their conversation. "Your Grace, you were saying you are in charge of the Christmas festivities at Avonmead this year?"

Annabel smiled and nodded, determined to proceed as the mistress of the estate, even if her absent husband never rejoined her. "Yes, Mrs. James, we have a wonderful event planned for all the tenants." Where was her blasted husband? Was he ever coming home?

~

"Four years ago, close to this time of the year, the baron called me into his study. It was the day I turned twenty-one. My ... birthday ..."

Philip wanted to stop the telling. He knew the baron was not a pleasant man, and how could a story that began with a birthday and ended with a familial estrangement possibly turn out well? Steeling his nerve, he reminded himself that he was here for Annabel's sake. He had hurt his wife, and he would make it up to her. No one had ever died because they were forced to listen to a tragic tale.

"... The baron felt that since I had now come of age, I was man enough to hear the truth. He no longer wanted a *snot-nosed brat* sitting across from him at his breakfast table every morning, so it was time for me to depart Baydon Hall. He informed me he was not my father, and we were not family. His brother, John Ridley, who died in a riding accident, had dishonored their family by getting his betrothed with child. There was to be a hurried wedding, but the baron—my true father—had taken a reckless ride to race a friend and had broken his neck in the subsequent fall just days before the wedding. As the new baron, he had been forced to salvage the family reputation by marrying—his words, not mine—the chit ... in other words, my mother. He was forced to take care of John Ridley's bastard brat and claim me as his own."

Philip rolled his head back to stare at the ceiling. He truly despised Filminster. Composing himself, he returned his gaze to his storyteller, who was staring sightlessly toward the mullioned window that looked out to the street. Philip waited for the man to resume.

"He let me know in no uncertain terms that this matter would remain a secret and he would not deny me as his heir, for my mother had failed to grant him a true heir. However, now that I was of age, I was to leave Baydon Hall and never return. His man of business would continue to provide an allowance if I did nothing to embarrass his name, and I could have use of the family estates outside of the Hall. I was not to visit, nor write, as no one wanted or needed to hear from me. I asked him about Annabel, if I could say goodbye. He said why would I want to do that? We were not family."

The man before him looked defeated as he repeated the baron's words. Pain lined his young face and made him look older than his years. Philip waited in silence—his chest tight and his lungs strained at the exertion of drawing breath—for the future lord to complete his telling. He could not reconcile the baron's behavior with that of his own loving parents, who had always made time for him and encouraged him in his learning and confidence. He had been devastated at their unexpected loss, while Filminster had thrown his family connections away like rubbish.

Ridley finally turned his defensive eyes back to the duke. "So, as you can see, our relationship is a lie, built on lies. Annabel and I are nothing to each other."

Philip frowned as he thought about the younger man's story. Ridley seemed sincere in his statement and did not appear to notice any illogic in his words.

The duke cleared his throat while he considered how to enlighten the future heir to Baydon Hall. "The baron is despicable, and your tale is ... heartbreaking. Which leaves me with the awkward position of ... I am unsure how to break this news to you ..." Philip attempted to gather his thoughts for clarity as he ventured to speak once more. "... but that makes Annabel your half-sister. Not to mention your cousin. But mostly your sister. And as your sister, she misses you and she needs you."

"Have you not listened to a word I said? We are not related! I have no connections of my own. I am a charity case along with my departed mother!"

Philip heard anguish in the man's voice and, in a sudden flash, comprehended what the other man had experienced. Brendan Ridley had been shaken to his core by the news the baron had imparted. He must have felt the disavowal so deeply that he had lost all sense of family and identity. Philip could understand the man's pain because of his own experiences with his late wife. As Annabel had once told him, some things needed to be said out loud, so they did not get stuck in one's skull to bounce around until they became disturbed and illogical. The man in front of him had convinced himself that he had no family and was lost in his dark thoughts, with no one to guide him out.

Which meant that Philip needed to intervene. Reason it out for the man. For Annabel.

"Have you spoken to anyone on this matter?"

"No one is aware. Saunton knows the baron threw me out of Baydon Hall, but not why."

"Brendan, do you mind if I call you Brendan?"

The younger man showed his assent, so Philip continued. "Brendan, your sister loves you very much. I can assure you that the fact of Filminster's brother being your true sire will make not a whit of difference to her. You are her brother, and that is all she cares about. You *are* connected to her—to *us*. Annabel loves you and misses you, and *we* are your family. You are important to her, to us ... to me ... brother."

Brendan started at this sentiment, looking at him with a wounded expression. To see such pain in the brandy eyes that looked just like Annabel's cut Philip to the core as he recalled how he had left his beautiful wife weeping in her chambers several days past.

"Brother?"

"Indeed. There is no man who can substitute for you, Brendan Ridley, and only *you* will do. Come what may, you *are* Annabel's brother, and she ... *we* need you in our lives."

The man swallowed hard, pressing his fist to his mouth with eyes closed as he drew a deep breath, the air thick with emotion. After several moments, he opened his eyes, and it was as if a storm had passed, for their depths were lit to reveal rich golds and browns. It was like staring into *her* eyes, and Philip had to fight back a wave of regret as he realized how much he missed his wife.

Ridley spoke. "What do you need?"

∾

Annabel was at her wit's end. Would the duke ever return? Where was he? Perhaps she was destined to walk the halls of Avonmead alone until the very end of her confinement.

The Halmesbury doctor who had visited had been an old man with white locks and balding pate. Quite jovial, the old man had confessed he was very busy in their underserved community. He had told her of an eminently competent midwife in the area who he thought might reside at Avonmead during Annabel's confinement, if the woman would be permitted to continue assisting the villagers. Annabel had reflected on the idea for the past several days, and she had determined it to be ideal. She liked the idea of a midwife over a doctor, and she had heard somewhere that they enjoyed a higher percentage of successful births. It stood to reason. Midwives delivered more babies than doctors did and would be more considerate of the trials of women.

Her mind made up, she walked down the first-floor hall toward the servants' entrance to locate Mrs. Harris. She could ring, but Annabel needed the distraction and exercise now that she had determined she should not ride the estate in her current condition. She reached the door and unlatched the handle to step into the dim corridor beyond, then jumped in surprise to hear raised voices once more. This time she could recognize Clinton's voice.

"You harridan of a miserable old woman! Will you not cooperate with the simplest request?"

"Your requests are not simple, unlike you!"

"It is how we have always handled matters at Avonmead. Just do it this way and stop your incessant arguing!"

"You stop your incessant arguing, you old codger! I am the housekeeper, and it is my decision!"

"Why, you—"

Annabel drew the door shut, cutting off any further arguing from reaching her. She thought about what she had heard in puzzlement until her lips curved up—she knew what she had borne witness to.

As she felt her face split into a smile, a chuckle escaped her lips. She had finally found an amusing distraction from her tribulations. Life was full of challenges, but it went on. Her life would go on, no matter what the future brought, and she would make the best of it.

CHAPTER
TWENTY-ONE

"What can stop the determined heart and resolved will of man?"

Mary Shelley's Frankenstein

~

Annabel looked around the nursery that had not been used in nearly two decades. It was … nice. It was clear that Philip and Sebastian's parents had not locked them away and forgotten them as some peers did, bringing their children out only as long as they were clean and well-behaved for a quick visit with the adults before rushing them back to the nursery. What would have happened to Annabel if not for her mama and Mrs. Harris?

There was evidence of love here. Plenty of windows to let light in. Under the dust sheets, she could make out many bookcases. She walked over and lifted a sheet, sneezing at the cloud of dust. As she had suspected, the shelves were crammed with books, toys, and what looked like lesson objects. Many of the books were stories and served no purpose other than to entertain.

She had finally come up to see this space reserved for the Markham children. It was nine days since Philip's departure, seven since his midnight visit to take the carriage. For all she knew, she would give birth to her child before she saw the duke again. After much debate with herself, she had determined that she must start planning for the nursery and for a nanny to assist her. She could not sit around waiting any longer; she needed to take action.

If I want the future I envision for myself, I must make it happen. I shall just have to reach out and take what I want.

Taking action was how she had changed her fate to marry Philip, rather than being imprisoned in a marriage to feckless Richard.

Her reasoning had led her to walk around the manse, searching for the nursery. She walked over to the window and leaned her forehead against the glass to stare out at the woods.

Oh, Philip, will you not come home?

They could return to how they had been and pretend she had never said those stupid words. They would return to being just companions. Maybe he would hold her in his arms like he had done before. She would not expect anything more or ask for anything he was not willing to give. She wanted to be in his life.

Annabel straightened and dashed the tears from her cheeks. She had been a veritable watering pot for an entire week, but she had found another project to occupy her thoughts. She would work on the nursery, then one step at a time, she would prepare to be a mother.

Philip may have decided their marriage was a mistake and regret his choice of wife, but they could still have children, starting with this one. Children would give her a new purpose—someone to whom she could channel all her unrequited love—if he was determined to keep distance between them. Perhaps more than one babe in the future. If Philip never returned her love, she could still have plenty of love in her life.

Waiting for him to come home was tremendously exasperating. She wanted to throw things, cry, or howl at the firmament—perhaps crawl out of her skin, which itched with the frustration of things not said or resolved. She needed to know where he was, to have a proper conversation, and to settle this matter. Instead, she scoured the nursery and made plans.

∽

PHILIP'S EXCITEMENT mounted as the carriage turned to enter the stone gates of Avonmead. It felt like he had been away for a hundred years, rather than a mere nine days. He half expected his home to look different.

Stuff, he was tired! No wonder he had become so fanciful.

He rubbed his face with his hands to ease the weariness from traveling. As the carriage neared the mansion, his nerves tingled in accompaniment with his heightening excitement. What would he say when he saw Annabel? Did she even want to see him after he had been such a scoundrel? It was difficult to accept that his rakish cousin was the one to point out that he, Philip, had been a thoughtless cad. He would never take Annabel for granted again. He would tell her he loved her every day for the rest of their lives. They would improve the estate school together, and she would help him prepare his speeches for

Westminster—they would do so many great things together.

He wondered just how angry she would be when he finally reached her.

He felt like a nervous youth on the first day of school as he attempted to repair his cravat, but after two days of driving from London through to Avonmead, he was decidedly disheveled. Before he could hunt for Annabel, he would need to call for his valet and make an effort to clean up. What he needed to say to her was too important to appear like a bedraggled lout.

He sighed with impatience. Yet another delay before he could speak to his lovely wife.

∽

PHILIP SPED up the stairs to his chambers. As he made his way down the carpeted second-floor hall lined with detailed oil landscapes of Wiltshire, his footfalls became all but silent, with the rich weavings dampening his approach. It was the reason why, when he turned a bend in the hall, his butler Clinton and the new housekeeper did not hear his entrance.

"Witch!"

"Why ... why ... you old dog!" hissed the short, stout woman standing toe to toe with his tall, slim manservant, her chin raised in defiance. Clinton's eyes flared at the insult, and they glared at each other. Philip was just contemplating how to make his presence known in order to reach his rooms when right in front of him the two flew into each other's arms in an embrace, lips smacking loudly against lips. Philip winced and turned to avert his vision. His suspicions were confirmed, but he felt no triumph. It was ... repulsive. Not unlike a child discovering their parents kissing.

He cleared his throat to announce his presence and listened to the sounds of consternation behind him.

"Your—Your Grace!" sputtered Clinton, his voice pitching from two different heights as the servant bowed behind him. Philip refused to turn around. His eyes might look down the hall toward the staircase, but his mind could not unsee the two locked in passionate abandon.

"See here, Clinton, I know many households do not allow servants to marry, but it seems to me both you and Mrs. Harris are mature and valued retainers, so if you wish to marry while maintaining your positions, I will have no argument. In fact, we can discuss you taking one of the cottages close to the manor. However, I would appreciate if you took steps to address this ... tension between you so that I might travel my halls without the fear of encumbrance. What do you say, old chap?"

Clinton sounded awkward when he gave a muffled cough, presumably into a gloved fist. "I will discuss the matter with Mrs. Harris and let you know, Your Grace?"

"Splendid, Clinton. As you were—wait ... scratch that. On second thought, please remove yourselves from my corridor and send my valet with haste. Also, I need to bathe, but I am in a hurry ... have a footman bring warm water for my washstand. I need to meet with my duchess, and I would not care to find either of you out here to interrupt me again today."

"Of course, Your Grace. My apologies, Your Grace."

"No need to mention this again. Let me know of your decision. Continue on."

As amused as Philip may have been under ordinary circumstances, as matters stood, the servants' drama was just another delay to reaching Annabel. His frustration at their long parting was making his skin itch. He needed to see his wife!

~

Annabel gazed through the glass walls of the orangery. The air was pungent with the smell of exotic fragrances of dozens of blooming plants along the scaffolding on the back wall and of ripe oranges and citrus growing on the trees dotted around the corners and edges of the windowed room.

Although melancholy still dogged her heels, she had found little projects to do. She kept wondering what the future would bring. Would Philip still want her to accompany him to London and play at being his hostess—not that she had any knowledge for such an undertaking? Or would she remain here at the estate for the coming year? Would he be pleased with her when he learned she was with child, or would it be the perfect excuse to stay away from her and leave for Town? She hoped with all her heart he would forgive her. If not, she had so much love for Philip that she could pass on to a little boy with his intelligent, determined gaze and infectious laugh, or a little girl with his glorious golden curls and serious gray eyes, to fill the void in her very being.

Hearing footsteps on the brick walkway, she looked back, expecting Mary with her tea tray, which Annabel had been taking in the orangery, with its enclosed lawn and charming breakfast area, for the past week. She started when she saw Philip standing near her.

"Your Grace, you have returned." She stood and dropped a curtsy, holding back a grimace.

Faugh, Annabel! That was not an awkward and inappropriate greeting at all.

"Annabel." He nodded in greeting before taking steps to sit on the bench at her side. Annabel followed his cue and sank slowly back onto the bench.

He cleared his throat. "I wanted to thank you for the information you uncovered. Richard and I have patched up our relationship. I let him know he is not welcome in our household because of his actions against you, but I am glad we can become acquainted once more. It is … nice to have some sense of the fraternity we once shared."

She nodded in acknowledgment, guilt twisting her insides at how she had withheld the Debrett's entry from him and had not intended to tell him about it. She was happy they had reconciled, as she wanted Philip to be happy. *That is a lie. I want to go back to the time before he knew what a mistake he had made in marrying me.* She felt tears prickling and swallowed hard, looking away while she fought to hold them back.

"I am curious how long you knew?"

She entwined her fingers to control their shaking. "About two weeks," she choked out.

"Ah, about the time of the strange conversation regarding family ties. Why did you not inform me as soon as you discovered it?"

She flinched at the question. Brave and honest, indeed. Annabel thought about the future she had hoped for, the one where Philip grew to love her, and they became partners for life. Where he visited her every night and stayed until morning, with the laughter of their children filling their days. She knew that was out of the question now. Not only had he realized his mistake in marrying her, but she had betrayed his trust and put her own happiness before his by withholding the truth about Jane and her brother. An act of unforgivable unkindness.

She steeled her resolve. She may have not been brave and honest until now, but it was time to tell the truth with courage and see where it would take her.

"I was enjoying our time together, and I wanted nothing to change."

"Why would it have changed?"

"I knew the primary reason you wanted to marry me was because of what Richard had done to you and ... you would realize your mistake in choosing me as your w-wife." Her voice broke. She fought for control. "I am so sorry," she whispered hoarsely, unable to look at him.

"I was afraid you would say something like that. However, I am the one who should apologize."

Annabel shook her head in denial. "You did so much for me. I do not blame you for your desire to hurt Richard, and you rescued me from a marriage I did not want."

"Annabel, that is not what I am apologizing for. First, you make me sound heroic, magnanimous even. My motives were purely selfish, I assure you. But I digress. First, I have news ... of your brother."

Annabel squinted at him in surprise. "Brendan? What does he have to do with us?"

"Your brother was quite pleased to learn of our marriage—"

"He was?"

"Sweet, you will have to stop interrupting so I can tell you my news."

Annabel shot him a chastened but curious look. She had much she wanted to say to him, but the sudden change in subject to her brother befuddled her thinking. She was unsure what thread of the conversation to concentrate on, so she acquiesced and stayed silent.

"Brendan misses you very much—has missed you very much, and he wrote a missive to you ..."

Philip withdrew a folded paper from a pocket in his coat pocket and handed it over. Annabel reached out a trembling hand to grasp it. She felt overcome with emotions and fought back more tears as she gently unfolded the letter. The first she had received from Brendan Ridley in four long years.

My dearest Annabel,

Felicitations on your recent nuptials. Halmesbury seems like a good sort, and I was most pleased to make your new husband's acquaintance. We discussed the situation with our family, and he has made me see we could and should reunite. I have much to explain and the duke has agreed that he will allow me to make my explanations to you directly, so do not pester him to inform you of the details. I know you will be tempted, but the explanation must come from me, so leave the poor man alone, sis.

I have personal matters to take care of, but the duke has invited me to Avonmead for my birthday on November 25, so I will join you in your new home soon. I know it is some years since we celebrated the holidays together, but I would very much like to resurrect our family traditions this year, if that is acceptable to you. The festive season has been most challenging for me since our parting, and I look forward to spending it with you this year. The duke appears to think you would be highly receptive, if not elated, to do so.

Please know that I did not intend our estrangement to hurt you, and it is not a reflection of my sentiments toward you. I have and always will love you as my most cherished family, and I look forward to reuniting soon.

With all my love,
Brendan

Annabel felt tears streaming down her cheeks at these long-awaited words from her beloved brother. It mortified her to be showing such emotion, and she attempted to mop her face by turning away from the duke to pat the end of her shawl around her throbbing eyes. Her heart, encased in ice for days, unfroze like snow in warm sunlight as she comprehended the news. Brendan was coming. Here to Avonmead. To visit her!

"I—thank you!" she blurted out in gratitude before a horrifying thought occurred to her. "Wait! Are you getting rid of me? Did you orchestrate this meeting with Brendan to ease my exit?"

Philip's face fell, and he reached out to pull her into a fierce embrace. "Never! Annabel—never!" he repeated as he pressed urgent kisses to the crown of her head. "My darling, I arranged this for you because I wanted to make amends for my behavior. This is my apology to you. And my gratitude. I needed to reconcile with Saunton. It was such a relief to talk with him, to clear up our misunderstanding, that I wanted to do something for you. As I was in London, I felt I could not leave without uncovering the cause of your estrangement with your brother. I just could not believe that he did not want you in his life. Of course he would want to be in your life! You are delightful! I suspected there was an explanation and a resolution for you and Brendan. You helped me reunite with my family, and I … I just wanted to help you reunite with your family so you could experience that relief for yourself."

"But … but …" Annabel frowned her confusion. "Why do you feel you owe me an apology?"

"I owe you an apology for my cowardice. I could not face my true feelings, and I allowed you to believe that our marriage was a convoluted revenge plot because I did not have the maturity to tell you the truth. To tell you how a bold, vivacious woman entered my study and captivated me from the start. How when she told me she was betrothed, I was horribly disappointed, but then when she told me to whom and that she wanted to break the betrothal, that I was so, so relieved that I had all the justification I needed to take her for my own. So relieved that I immediately proposed rather than lose the opportunity to spend my time with the most beautiful, exciting woman I had ever encountered. How within a few days I was madly in love with this exquisite creature, and that when she told me she loved me, it squeezed my heart with joy, but I was too immature, too callow, too fearful to state my reciprocation of those treasured words out loud." Philip cleared his throat. "It is time I correct that—I love you, Annabel. Deeply. Passionately. These past few weeks have been the happiest weeks of my entire life. You are my new best friend and my beloved. I am so fortunate that you turned to me for help. I cannot possibly be happy without you at my side."

Annabel struggled to pull her head back to gape at him. "What?"

Philip chuckled. "I do not think I can repeat all that. I assume you are expressing surprise and not that you failed to hear what I said?"

"What?" Annabel's wits were dull with shock and happiness. She shook her head to clear her thoughts and then threw herself forward against his broad chest. "You love me? But I lied to you!"

"Not really. You simply withheld some facts, because you were uncertain of what my reception would be. And that, my dear, says more about my recent behavior than it does yours. If I had been more honest, then you would have had more confidence. In my newfound spirit of clarity, I can now honestly inform you that you are the most captivating woman I have ever met."

Annabel laughed in relief and buried her face against his tanned neck. "I know I promised to never say it again, but ... I love you, Philip."

"Hmm ..." He nuzzled her temple before using his hand to tilt her face up.

Annabel leaned back and playfully punched his shoulder with her fist. "You think it is that easy? I have been suffering from a broken heart, and I need to hear it again," she demanded.

"I love you. I love you! I love you, and I will always love you, Annabel. You complete me. How is that?"

"It is a good start."

Philip laughed as he stood up. Leaning down, he braced his arm to swing her knees up, and his other arm cradled her back lovingly as he scooped her up. He leaned down and planted a kiss on her lips.

"Oh, Philip, in the interest of honesty, I should inform you I had to begin preparations for the nursery."

He stumbled slightly and then righted himself. "What?"

"We are with child, My Grace."

"What?"

"I assume you did hear me and that you are merely expressing surprise?"

Philip gazed down at her before giving a whoop of happiness and lifting her higher with exultation. "A delightful surprise, my lovely Annabel. Delightful indeed!"

CHAPTER
TWENTY-TWO

"There is love in me the likes of which you can scarcely imagine."

Mary Shelley's Frankenstein

∽

It had taken three Sundays to have the banns read, which was how Brendan had come to arrive in time for the Monday morning wedding. They had enjoyed a glorious birthday breakfast on the morning of his arrival, with odd foods from the Ridley family culture that Annabel said she would explain. She had also promised Philip, with a serious countenance, that they would add their own Markham touches to the holiday traditions. He, in turn, had accused her of being too sentimental, but secretly it elated him to build and combine Markham traditions with those of the Ridley family.

After their breakfast, Philip had left the siblings to their private dialogue. As predicted, Annabel had not cared about the siring of Brendan Ridley. In fact, she had expressed her envy that Brendan could honestly claim he was no child of the baron. Later that afternoon, Philip asked with high hopes if that meant that they would no longer have to visit the baron, but Annabel had shaken her head at him. "We must be kind to the baron, Philip. He has no heart, and he has thrown his family connections away. Pity his poor choices and limit our interactions, but kind we must be. He is a man growing old, and we will be there for him even when he does not appreciate how difficult he makes it to spend time with him. Our generosity will pay back dividends in the form of an eased conscience and lightness of spirit because we did the right thing, My Grace."

Philip begrudgingly agreed to the value in her statements. Although he despised the baron, he would make the effort to maintain their relationship, but only to ensure Annabel's happiness.

The breakfast had marked the beginning of the festive rituals of Annabel's departed mother, and Philip had achieved his lifelong dream of the signs and sounds of family filling the halls of Avonmead. He enjoyed married life to Annabel as they found their rhythm, fitting their lives and interests together to form a new whole.

He and Brendan were forging their new relationship while Brendan and Annabel rediscovered their own.

Soon, she promised, they would all venture out to search for greenery and create Christmas boughs. The idea of partaking in an intimate family ritual had filled him with anticipation. He had missed all the holiday family activity since his mother had passed away in his youth.

Everywhere he looked, it was coming up family, as he watched the couple at the front. His wife had insisted on plaiting red ribbons through the bride's graying brown hair, and the groom loomed over her with an expression that could only be described as ... lighthearted?

As the ceremony proceeded in the quaint Avonmead chapel, Philip leaned over to place his gloved hand over Annabel's. They shared the pew with her brother as they faced the altar and listened to the lugubrious vicar intone the solemn vows. "Mabel Harris, will you have this man to be your husband; to live together in the covenant of marriage? Will you love him, comfort him, honor and keep him, in sickness and in health; and, forsaking all others, be faithful to him as long as you both shall live?"

"I will," stated the bride, her hazel eyes glowing as she stared up at her groom.

Annabel leaned over and whispered in his ear, "Mrs. Harris has a first name! And it's Mabel? How did I never know that?"

"Shhh ... do not interrupt Clinton's vows," he teased as he breathed onto the shell of her ear, causing her to shiver in a delightful manner. As they sat, hand in hand, witnessing his butler and her housekeeper wed, Philip reflected on how much his life had changed since his audacious wife had stolen into his study ... and his heart. He would be forever thankful that his cousin, his great friend, was an incorrigible libertine who had set a series of events into motion, resulting in Philip's eternal happiness. To share his life with Annabel, to voice his thoughts out loud to a true partner so they never again got stuck in his head, to share a genuine connection with another person ... he was truly blessed.

To Philip's added delight, and in the spirit of family and holidays, a second wedding breakfast would be held at Avonmead two days hence, which he looked forward to as it had been a long time coming, and Mrs. Thorne deserved to find her happiness after such a long wait. Not to mention that the young woman would finally be able to live under her true name. When the two of them had struck their bargain in July 1815, he could never have predicted how long it would take for it all to get sorted out.

He sighed in contentment as he squeezed Annabel's slim fingers. She was well pleased with his decision to allow his butler and her favorite housekeeper to wed while maintaining their positions. His wife had confided that she had long suspected a love match was afoot after encountering the two servants hissing and yelling at each other on several occasions.

Philip realized he should pay attention to the ceremony, as his thoughts were wandering. Squeezing his wife's hand, he gently placed it back in her lap, folded his arms, and made a concerted effort to concentrate on the couple getting married at the front of the chapel.

EPILOGUE

"You must create a female for me."

Mary Shelley's Frankenstein

~

1820, EARLY SPRING

Philip folded his paper as he peered over at his wife. Annabel had a delightful habit of humming with enjoyment when she ate buttered toast, and the sounds were distracting him. They had finally made it to London together, and it was a splendid time of the year to be introducing Annabel to its delights. The weather was pleasant, the cherry trees were blooming and, according to the paper, hell had frozen over.

"Annabel?"

"Hmm ... yes, My Grace?"

"Could I have your full attention, or are you planning to

run away with that toast and leave me to raise our son without you?"

"There is a thought."

Philip laughed as he reached to swipe his thumb over the dab of butter on the corner of her lower lip. "Love, I would prefer you do not joke about that." He raised his thumb to his mouth and licked it clean.

"I did not. You were the one who made the jest."

"Honey, I am serious. Pay attention, I have news to impart."

Annabel turned her glorious brandy eyes to his, causing him to pause in fascination.

"News?" she queried.

"Our timing in finally bringing you to London is ... serendipitous. It appears you will soon be able to meet the *Countess* of Saunton."

Annabel's jaw dropped. "Saunton is ... *married*?"

"Indeed, the papers report he shared his nuptials with a delightful Miss Sophia Hayward who was on her fourth Season."

"Who is she?"

"I have no idea. But she is an uncommonly brave young woman, I would say."

Annabel smiled as she looked back at her favored toast, eyeing the melting butter with evident relish. "Indeed. There must be quite a story to how that match came about."

Philip smiled as he gently disagreed. "Not as interesting as our own story, my sweet Annabel."

"Indeed, husband. I look forward to continuing our story when you take me to visit the pelicans in St. James's Park with our son this afternoon."

Philip groaned. "Pelicans? You will turn me into a veritable Dr. Syntax, visiting every picturesque tourist spot in the city!"

"Well ... I have never seen a pelican, and it sounds more interesting than attending obligatory dos with pompous peers to forward your political aims. Just be grateful I do not plan to sketch *every* spot we will visit," Annabel rejoined with a impudent smirk.

Philip shook his head in resignation before leaning down to press a firm kiss to her plump, buttery lips. "You are an autocrat, wife, but I will concede that it is only fair we go view your wildlife before you accompany me to the Russian ambassador's soiree tonight to commence mingling with my wildlife."

Annabel giggled nervously. "Please do not remind me that my duchess studies are about to be assayed by the Russian countess herself."

"She would not dare cross me ... and you will win her heart just as you have won mine, Annabel. You are an original."

Annabel blushed with pleasure as she stretched up to return his kiss.

∽

Curious if a rake like Lord Richard Balfour could redeem himself, fix his past misdeeds, and find true love? Find out in Miss Hayward and the Earl!

AFTERWORD

Annabel and Philip's story is inspired by my real-life courtship and wedding to my wonderful husband over eighteen years ago. There was no cheating fiancé, but there was a painful parting with a longtime boyfriend just before we met.

When I met Mr. Jarrett, I knew he differed from any man I had met before and our love developed quickly. When he proposed, it was a simple decision to accept. Which was how we married—fifteen days after we met—on an icy winter's night, surrounded by friends, which included one or two marriage officers as luck would have it.

We married in Illinois, rather than St. Louis, because there was a three day waiting period in Missouri, but we could obtain our own "special license" in Illinois, which only requires a single day.

It was the best decision I ever made and we have never looked back. However, marrying so quickly introduces unique challenges such as those experienced by Annabel and Philip.

AFTERWORD

I hope you enjoyed my first novel and stay tuned to learn how Richard Balfour attempts to redeem himself to pursue a more honorable path in *Miss Hayward and the Earl*.

∽

Stay in touch by signing up for the C. N. Jarrett newsletter!

About the Author

C. N. Jarrett started writing her own stories in elementary school but got distracted when she finished school and moved on to non-profit work with recovering drug addicts. There she worked with people from every walk of life from privileged neighborhoods to the shanty towns of urban and rural South Africa.

One day she met a real-life romantic hero. She instantly married her fellow bibliophile and moved to the USA where she enjoyed a career as a sales coaching executive at an Inc 500 company. She lives with her husband on the Florida Gulf Coast.

Jarrett believes in kindness and the indomitable power of the human spirit. She is fascinated by the amazing, funny people she has met across the world who dared to change their lives. She likes to tell mischievous tales of life-changing decisions and character transformations while drinking excellent coffee and avoiding cookies.

Stay in touch by signing up for the C. N. Jarrett newsletter!

Also by C. N. Jarrett

DAZZLING DEBUTANTES

Book 1: Miss Ridley and the Duke

Book 2: Miss Hayward and the Earl

Book 3: Miss Davis and the Spare